Stephen Watson Fullom

The exile's Daughter

A Story of the Italian War

Stephen Watson Fullom

The exile's Daughter
A Story of the Italian War

ISBN/EAN: 9783743357082

Manufactured in Europe, USA, Canada, Australia, Japa

Cover: Foto ©Andreas Hilbeck / pixelio.de

Manufactured and distributed by brebook publishing software (www.brebook.com)

Stephen Watson Fullom

The exile's Daughter

THE

EXILE'S DAUGHTER.

.

A Story of the Italian War.

By S. W. FULLOM,

AUTHOR OF

"THE GREAT HIGHWAY," "THE MARVELS OF SCIENCE,"
"THE HUMAN MIND," ETC., ETC.

LONDON:

CHARLES JOSEPH SKEET,

KING WILLIAM STREET, CHARING CROSS.

1860.

PREFACE.

A VISIT to the Sub-Alpine Kingdom during the war presented the country to me in so picturesque a light, and the people, animated by patriotism, in an aspect so different from that exhibited by the populations of the South, that, on returning home, I felt a desire to record my impressions; and, having given them publicity as a journalist, in this volume I submit them as an author.

With respect to the terrorism in Naples, I have sought rather to subdue, than deepen the colouring, and though the picture is still too dark, I have but feebly depicted the facts. For the story itself I can offer no apology. It may be thought, on a first view, that the perilous journey of the heroine with the intercepted despatch verges on the improbable; but, though I was not aware of the fact at the time, such a service, as a glance at the "Notes" will show, was actually performed, under circumstances somewhat similar, but still more romantic, by a young lady of eighteen. So difficult is it for fiction to match the strangeness of truth!

S. W. F.

Tudor Villa, Surbiton,
  March, 1860.

CONTENTS.

PART THE SIXTH.

PART THE SEVENTH.

PART THE EIGHTH.

THE LAND OF TERROR.

In fair Palermo is a street

Where two highways, like rivers, meet

  Before a pile of stone,

A pile that has its windows barred,

And at its massive door a guard,

  Who paces there alone—

His firelock charged, and on it set

A naked, gleaming bayonet:

Its evil shadow might one trace,

A scowl presents it on his face.

Night—such a night as southern clime

Affords to summer in its prime—

A twilight tint, like daylight pale,

That covers Nature with a veil,

Though, like a daughter of the isle,

She partly shows her face the while,

So languishing, so charming made ,

By the soft voluptuous shade—

With stars by thousands spread above,

The jewels in her crown of love,

And on her breath, so light and free,

The fragrance of the land and sea.

Fallen had such a night around,

Like a shower on desert ground,

Diffusing, lieu of fervid heat,

A zephyr soft, and odours sweet;

And one looked for a gladsome crowd

To roam about with voices loud,

And balconies with windows wide,

Where maids would stand their swains beside;

From every house a stream of light,

To give a welcome to the night,

And strains of music on the air,

And full enjoyment everywhere.

But there rose up the pile of stone,

And there still paced the guard alone,

   With murder in his eye—

And a spell of fear was thrown

   On every passer-by:

And each went on with noiseless tread,

As in a city of the dead—

For such, I ween, it might have been,

From the silence overhead.

Not a note of music or song,

No window wide the street along,

No streaming lights, no open door,

With neighbours gossiping before,

Nor graceful maids nor lovers by

To whisper, rally, smile, and sigh,

But only those few straggling folk,

  Who onward crept apart,

Each with the weight of a tyrant's yoke

  Pressed down upon his heart.

Broke suddenly upon the ear

A sound might well awaken fear,

The measured tramp and clang of arms

That heralds soldiers and gendarmes;

And, swift as sparks in airy flight,

The stragglers all escaped from sight.

One could not tell, so quick they fled,

Or how or whither they had sped,

But like a field by reapers mown,

Before a minute's space had flown,

All silent was the street and lone.

And on the iron column came,

Athirst with fury as a flame,

As eager to devour:

The blazon of a monarch's shame,

The sceptre of his power,

And night and day, the same array

Paraded each frequented way,

     At an unlooked-for hour.

Men turned uneasy in their bed

At sound of the familiar tread,

And many, as they shrinking lay,

Recalled each action of the day,

If by a word, or by a look,

They aught of licence once had took,

Or, by a gesture of dissent,

Betrayed they were not quite content,

And, under provocation hard,

One moment wavered from their guard.

And some there were—*sospetti* named,

By power branded as untamed,

For though they ne'er had swerved beyond

The strictest letter of the bond,

Nor edicts nor the laws had broke,

But silent bore the galling yoke;

Their thoughtful eyes divulged a look,

A despot's minions could not brook.

They met their frown with steady nerve,

Sheathed in the armour of reserve;

And treason, not in words expressed,

Alarms more deeply in the breast:

So, like caged beasts, that ne'er can fly

The keeper's overruling eye,

These all had an attendant spy,

Who met their glance, with gaze intent,

Where'er they turned, where'er they went:

And, such a shadow on the soul,

They felt no dread of the patrol;

For seizure, bondage—death, in brief—

Compared with this, had been relief.

Man may evade, or may defy,

Or, in enduring, bravely die,

And, optional to shun or meet,

We may do battle or retreat;

But woman, though not made to dare,

Her lot, whate'er it be, must bear;

Nor that alone, but, with her own,

Our burden and our griefs must share!

Her gentle heart, so prompt to feel,

It need be panoplied in steel,

Accessible at every pore,

Is open to its inmost core,

Yet, moulded for a great design,

Is gifted with a strength divine,

And not till trial, not till strain,

Knows the whole weight it can sustain:

So, in the hour of fortune's strife,

She is the spirit of our life,

And by a thousand holy ties,

Which then invisibly arise—

By those endearing sympathies,

That double and renew our powers,

Her being is absorbed in ours.

We bear the wound, she feels the pang,

She cheers us 'mid the battle's clang,

And when we seek the couch of rest,

She is the warder of our breast—

A sentinel before the camp,

Whose ardour no fatigue can damp!

And now, in many dwellings round,

Such loving watchers might be found,

Who, on their pillow, were alert

Surprise or peril to avert;

At any movement in the street,

Springing in terror to their feet,

And listening with acutest sense,

In a wild tremor of suspense:

For none could tell where would be made

The domiciliary raid,

Whose husband, father, brother, son,

The fierce police might pounce upon;

And to their den bear swift away,

As a tiger does its prey.

There was a chamber wide and dark,

With walls of stone, antique and stark,

But showing, in devices quaint,

Now mutilate by time, and faint,

The vestiges of bygone state,

That made it look more desolate—

A chamber old, and grim and cold,

That once had known a brighter fate,

But, through vicissitudes untold,

Had come with misery to mate—

Here, 'mid the deep pervading gloom,

That hung in shadows round the room,

Near a dim lamp, whose waning light

Broke like a glowworm on the sight,

There sat a maid, so rapt, so still,

So like the breath of sculptor's skill,

Save that o'er every feature stole

The beams of an unspotted soul,

Her head just bent, her eyes askance—

She seemed a spirit in a trance.

Her brow shone out more dazzling fair

Beneath a mass of raven hair,

And circling gold and sparkling gem

Could not enrich that diadem:

With the soft lustre of her eye

The rarest jewels could not vie;

For, in their flood of jetty light,

They fused the morning with the night;

And o'er her face their glances clear

Expanded as an atmosphere.

Quick as a bird the tramp she heard

Of the coming, common foe—

The sound she'd bitter cause to know;

And one might all her feelings trace

In the expression of her face:

Emotions of conflicting hue,

Each a distinct reflection threw,

And as a prism will display

The varied tints of a single ray,

So one sad look reflected there

Dread, anguish, horror, hate, despair.

She hastily put out the lamp—

For like a curfew was that tramp,

Without its monitory knell;

And darkness rose on every side,

Where'er its dreaded echo fell—

A darkness with itself allied,

To do the ministry of hell,

And through the blind, in shadow cast,

She watched till the gendarmes had passed;

Then o'er her head a mantle threw,

And to the door in tremor flew.

It opened on a dismal stair—

  The highest landing;

And the moon, through skylight spare,

  In beams expanding,

Cast its light where she was standing:

But the old staircase, all around,

The summit downward to the ground,

Was swathed throughout in gloom profound;

And through the house reigned silence deep,

No breath disturbed its midnight sleep,

Though every floor, in the descent,

Was rented as a tenement,

And, fallen from its ancient state,

Comprised a household separate.

Awhile in reverie she stood,

As though her purpose held not good;

And from this summit glancing down,

Fortune, in truth, might seem to frown,

And meet her there, upon the stair,

Donning the moonlight as a crown,

While darkness, like a wizard's shroud,

Enveloped it in folds of cloud,

So that it seemed for her to wait—

Not as Fortune, but as Fate.

Nor did she from herself conceal

What perils round her path might steal,

And, with a tiger-spring, attack,

As she, unguarded, turned her back—

Beside the danger manifest,

That, like a cordon, would invest;

For not a step could she advance

Protected from an ambushed glance,

As every house was full of spies,

And here the very walls had eyes,

While in the streets, in each dark nook,

Murder and Theft their station took,[1]

By royal licence free to act,

The town to harass and distract.

And when she looked the staircase down,

Meeting her gaze with such a frown—

Thought of the corridors unseen,

And saw the looming depth between,

Her heart for one brief moment sunk,

As from the enterprise it shrunk,

But quickly, like a champion hale,

It donned again its suit of mail,

And darting down, as arrow fleet,

She reached the hall and gained the street.

No demoiselle of high degree,

Nor cradled child of fortune she:

Her father was an advocate,

A man of honourable fame,

But 'mongst his fellows claiming weight

More by his learning than estate,

And by his old untarnished name:

And she, commended to his care,

By her dead mother's latest prayer,

Had grown and bloomed his heart beside,

His hope, his treasure, and his pride.

Alas! the inauspicious hour!—

She charmed the eye of brutal power:

A tyrant's tool, a subtle knave,

Himself a recreant and slave,

Had sought to link her honest name

With his opprobrium and shame.

By sire and maiden he was spurned,

And kindled hate where love had burned,

A hate that, with consuming fire,

Aimed to destroy both maid and sire.

'Twas midnight when its fury broke,

And from her slumbers Lilla woke:

An instinct, as by Heaven sent,

A warning and presentiment,

Like angel breathing in her ear,

Divined and shaped the danger near;

And ere she reached her father's room,

She knew its author and his doom—

Knew he had been condemned unheard

On Branti's unsupported word;

And they had roused him from his sleep

To bear him to a dungeon deep.

Though thronged by the spectators base,

She sprang with sobs to his embrace,

Nor would unloose her clinging arms,

Till dragged away by the gendarmes.

As by its clement sovereign liege

The city was declared in siege,

So now upon this household fell

The midnight visit like a shell;

And each domestic, from his bed,

Half-dressed, obeyed the summons dread,

And mustered, trembling, on the stair,

Beneath the torch's vivid glare,

Where the police might fiercely scan,
If any dared to look a man.

And thus, in insolent array,
They tore their prisoner away:
Fetters and gyves his limbs restrain,
And bind him with their felon chain;
But still his voice—that voice so dear—
O'er all the din, reached Lilla's ear,
And in his last half-uttered word,
His love and her own name she heard.

Unnoticed from the house she stole,
In the devotion of her soul;
And through the street, the city through,
Still kept in sight the ruffian crew—

With aching, breaking, panting heart,

That seemed as if 'twould rend apart,

And flitting through surrounding night,

Like self-illumined aërolite.

And when they reached the prison door,

The fountains of her life-blood froze;

She saw them pass its threshold o'er,

And then the iron portal close—

　She saw no more!

Her senses seemed to come and go,

As surging waves recede ànd flow,

But, as these leap their bounds at last,

And sweep in flood expansive past,

So, in a while, her aching brain

Was 'lumined by its tide again.

And then there rose a sudden fear

That Branti might be hovering near.

Or, in the home his vengeful hate

Had made so drear and desolate,

Expecting her return, might wait:

And came a thought, as 'twere a gleam

Of some remote, forgotten dream,

That throws up objects dim and faint—

Of a sequestered house, and quaint,

A mansion, in a suburb lone,

With stories five of chiselled stone,

Defaced and blurred, as by a curse,

Where dwelt a faithful friend, her nurse;

And, flying to this ancient lair,

She sought and found a refuge there.

Not since that hour, by night or day,

She'd from her chamber dared to stray,

And though her nurse made anxious quest,

So far as she might manifest,

No tidings of her father heard,

Nor of his fate a trace or word;

For once within those doors of doom,

There was the mystery of the tomb.

This night, by impulse tender urged,

She first from her retreat emerged,

For 'twas a night her sire and she,

In the bright time when they were free,

Had aye been wont to celebrate

As a great festival and *fête*,

Her name-day—to her honour given,

And to her patron saint's in Heaven!

Ah! 'twas a cruel, woful change

Such gladness for misfortune strange!

That day, so happy in the past,

All weary hours, from first to last;

The morning in deep gloom had risen,

And now she'd wandered to the prison.

There was the Criminalli[2] door,

She stood the frowning pile before,

Unnoted by the sentinel—

For round the spot a shadow fell,

As 'twere a cloak invisible,

And, thus begirt, her spirit passed,

Through door and grate and postern fast,

And, on its sacred purpose bent,

Into her father's dungeon went.

But 'twas not given to descry,

Through granite walls, with Fancy's eye,

Or to conceive, with brain of fire,

The secrets of that prison dire;

And of the labyrinth of stone

To Lilla not a glimpse was shown.

Horrors arose to her rapt eyes,

But, oh! the truth might paralyze!

For though appeared no softening gleam,

To break the darkness of her dream,

And penetrate, a stifled ray,

The narrow vault where her father lay—

The narrow vault, so like a tomb

In its impenetrable gloom,

And he within, a captive lone,

Who daily wasted to the bone,

A skeleton, but with life's pains,

His limbs still locking in their chains.

No eye could lift the curtain fell

That masked from view this earthly hell.

While by such fancied horrors swayed,

A hand was on her shoulder laid,

And through her frame a tremor broke

As when a somnambulist is 'woke,

And sees in front a deep abyss,

Her foot upon the precipice—

For, turning quickly, she espied

The dreaded Branti at her side.

"Ah, Lilla! signorina sweet,

This is a rendezvous most meet!

The silence round, the midnight hour,

Yon charming fabric for a bower—

Methought I'd be a watcher near,

When Love should guide your footsteps here:

So, nightly taking up my station,

At last I've won an assignation:

And, 'fore the pontiff moon above,

I now can pay my vows of love

And tributary adoration!"

The sting that barbed his mocking speech

Her tempered spirit failed to reach,

But he, the scorpion, could feel

Her scorn was like a crushing heel;

And as, before her piercing glance,

This spasm surprised his countenance,

*

The terrors of his evil might,

Seemed like a mist to pass from sight,

And seeing what an abject thing

Was this reflection of a king,

She felt 'twere shame in her to cower,

When but her fear would give him power.

And yet his words, his presence there,

Brought a conviction of despair;

For they confirmed her deep belief

He was the author of her grief—

That 'twas for her, and her alone,

Her sire was in a dungeon thrown,

And when she might avert this fate,

What course did duty's voice dictate?

Alas! 'twas terrible to think,

But, for his sake, she would not shrink.

" If 'twas to mock me, and to jeer,

You waited to confront me here,

The will divine that I obeyed

Brought me not hither to upbraid :

Ere now you've told me that you love,

And called to witness saints above,

And if those spirits you revere,

If e'er, in truth, you held me dear,

Then, for my weal—your own—abate

This burst—this triumph of your hate.

In thraldom that all hope denies,

My father in yon prison lies—

I ask not by whose stern decree,

But you—your word can set him free !"

Then curled derisively his lip,

Meeting his glance in fellowship,

A lurid glance, that gave a light

As it flashed out upon the night;

And on his face, as on a scroll,

Revealed the instincts of his soul:

So, where the thunder-clouds are riven,

Darts out the lightning swift from Heaven,

And shows, to the horizon's bound,

Darkness, darkness all around.

" His dungeon I can open throw—

His bonds knock off, and bid him go—

Would you but tell me what I know?

Or is this cue, this hint astute,

Proud Lilla's notion of a suit?"

" If suit will move your hand to save,

With burning tears the boon I'll crave;

O! let it be a suit, a prayer,

If you will yield, if you will spare."

"Howe'er accustomed to subdue

'Tis plain you know not how to sue :

Not prayers alone, nor pleading tone,

Nor a bewailing damsel's moan

Will, like an Ariadne's clue,

Thread for your sire an avenue

  Through yonder maze of stone.

Prayers moved not you in your strong hour :

Is Beauty more austere than Power ?

Like Love, so Mercy has its price,

And Justice claims a sacrifice :

So, if you would your suit obtain,

In this wise plead, or plead in vain !"

"O! to redeem him from that hold,

I'd give, wer't mine, his weight in gold."

"Your liberality in speech

I would not for the world impeach;

But, since the gold will surely fail,

Enter yourself the empty scale!

O! you demur! Take time to muse,

He perishes, if you refuse!

A few brief days of fever o'er,

They'll ope, indeed, his prison door,

Not to commute or waive his doom

But to consign him to the tomb."

From Lilla broke a bitter cry—

'My father in his bonds to die!

O! save him—give him back to life,

And I will be your faithful wife!"

"I'm less exacting than you'd own—"

She shrank at his caressing tone—

"Nor would on your fresh youth impose

The galling bondage wedlock throws.

No, let some more encroaching swain

Condemn you to that servile chain.

I ask what you may lightly give—

Then yours to say your sire shall live;

For morning's dawn shall set him free,

Pay you before his ransom fee!"

A moment Lilla speechless stood,

O'erborne by passion's rushing flood;

But soon her words like ripples came,

Above that ferment of her blood:

"Destroyer of my home and name!"

She said, in tones by depth subdued,

"To me you dare propose this shame!

Your villany I will proclaim—

The whole—my cause, my father's, bring,

Through all his guards, before the king."

"And from his court with stripes be driven!"

Too sure this issue to deny,

She pointed to the starlit sky—

"There is a King in Heaven!"

So beautiful in form and face,

Her faith conferred a higher grace;

And Branti, in his evil might,

Recoiled before her arm of light.

'Twas but, indeed, a passing qualm,

He knew how powerless that arm!

And Superstition's voice was weak

Where Nature's self had ceased to speak.

"My king's on earth, my Heaven here,

And you the only angel near:

My prize, my spoil, I'll not resign"—

He caught her round—"You shall be mine!"

But with a bound, and with a cry,

She struggled to escape and fly,

And, ere he could a footstep note,

A hand athletic grasped his throat—

A hand that seems with iron strung,

And headlong to the ground he's flung.

"Assassin!" still half stunned, he cried,

"Meet now the fate you have defied!"

He snatched a dagger from his vest

And flew at his assailant's breast.

"Madonna, thou his buckler now!"

And Lilla could not check a scream

At the uplifted blade's bright gleam,

So swiftly, madly darting by,

Like the flash of a wrathful eye.

But as a gallant ship and free,

Beset upon a stormy sea,

Rides o'er the toppling rushing wave,

That threatened to become its grave,

Her champion the onset breasts,

And, closing in, the dagger wrests—

Then, threw it high above his head,

And Branti, worsted, turned and fled.

The sentinel had heard the din,

And roused the sleeping guard within,

And, from the portal of the gaol,

A torch threw a reflection pale,

As if, such darkness left behind,

The night, by dazzling, smote it blind.

" Ah, fly!" cried Lilla, "yet I claim

To know my brave deliverer's name!"

But not a moment left to say

He but replied—" Away! away!"

And as the guard came bounding on

He waved adieu—and she was gone!

THE PRISON.

Go back to times when feudal power

Intrenched itself in keep and tower,

When barons fierce, and robber bands,

Exacted spoil with iron hands,

When might was right, and right was wrong,

The will ungoverned of the strong,

Religion but the pillar of cloud,

And Justice by its terrors cowed,

And guided by the ordeal's glance,

The senseless oracle of Chance.

When Letters slept, and Art was dead,

And monk-craft flourished in their stead—

There still, in this appalling night,

Were traces of redeeming light,

Emitting many a twinkling ray,

Like an encircling Milky Way:

And Troubadours, with lyre and song,

And ladies fair, with love's soft tongue,

And priests, advancing in the van,

Preserved humanity to man.

But now we live in broadest day,

All earth—and Heaven—may survey:

No islets in the ocean lie,

No stars in the remotest sky,

But they are pictured to the eye:

Religion, bursting forth entire,

Is once again the pillar of fire:

Art now has Nature's power won,

And a new province through the sun,

That, like a viceroy, bears her sway,

Where brush or pencil ne'er can stray;

The fluid lightning hastes to flow,

As Science bids it come and go;

Nor lightning nor the sun is seen

Where Literature has not been,

And small dominion claims the sword,

When rules the Press as sovereign lord!

Yet this illuminated age,

Whose range and grasp we scarce can gauge,

Still looks upon benighted climes,

A remnant of the heritage

That comes to us from ancient times.

Behold o'er Freedom's heights the morn

With radiance the sky adorn,

While in the valleys, just below,

Still frowning rocks their shadows throw!

Where Etna and Vesuvius rise

No realm so fair beneath the skies:

Yet in this Eden, man, a thrall,

Has undergone a second Fall,

And while on every side is light,

Here is the deep eclipse of night,

So that barbaric life is found

Enclosed in civilization's bound,

And casts a blot upon the age

That else were History's brightest

Here Justice is a labelled name,

Which suitors buy, and rulers shame,

Each functionary, in his sphere,

A satrap and a buccaneer;

And, linked in an unbroken chain

Not one, ten thousand tyrants reign!

O'er rich and poor, o'er high and low,

The same oppressive yoke they throw,

Till all succumb, from daily use,

To Power's utmost, worst abuse,

And by their abject terror bring

A stigma on the name of king.

Ah, Sicily! enchanting isle,

Spread on the waters like a smile,

How oft I've scanned thy varied shore,

Arising now as through a haze,

The fading hues that Time throws o'er—

As 'twould elude fond memory's gaze,

And veil the scenes of other days;

Yet still I see tall Etna's cone,

Majestically raised alone,

O'erlooking the fair island round,

And the bright sea that forms its bound,

And challenging th' exalted skies,

Like Lucifer in Paradise!

And many a bluff cliff I trace,

All furrowed like a seaman's face;

And many a slope with verdure dressed,

Heaving up like a gentle breast;

And olives, vines, and orange-trees,

Yielding sweet incense to the breeze.

Yet not for these I love thee most,

Although of these thou well mayst boast—

Nor for thine old and hallowed glory,

Embalmed in chronicle and story,

Nor for when Error ruled the earth,

Thou gavest Archimedes birth,.

With dying flash, supremely bright,

To latest ages throwing light:

I love thee for thy sons are brave,

And oft have sought a freeman's grave,

And, oh! still more our love they claim,

As dear to them is England's name,

And, let but time propitious be,

We'll claim, sweet isle, redress for thee!

How sharp the agony of wrong,

That Lilla's gentle bosom wrung!

D

The angel who to heaven bears

Devotion's thanks, and sorrow's prayers,

Receiving such a cry of woe,

With tears and fears o'erladen so,

Must feel a sympathetic throe:

And, as she met his pitying sight,

Would quicken heavenward his flight

To lay her soul-inspired appeal

Where men and angels both must kneel.

Her father, as from Branti fell—

She pictured in a noisome cell,

On fever's raging surges tost—

Alone, untended, dying, lost!

Could she his head one moment raise,

And he but meet her loving gaze,

The gaze he oft, so oft, had sought—

O! there was ransom in the thought!

For 'twould to him such solace bring,

Death would, she knew, lose half its sting,

And scarce the Church's shriving voice

His parting soul would more rejoice.

For such a moment, such an end,

The balance of her life she'd spend,

Nor ask from him one last caress,

But simply with a look to bless!

Like a delusion—undefined—

The project seized upon her mind,

But by degrees, with vigour rife,

Took range and outline, form and life:

Then, quick she fashioned a disguise

That might delude a gaole'rs eyes:

And masks her mission, yet declares
The garb a Sister of Mercy wears.

She knows the risk and peril great,
But not the horrors that await:
A hero's courage she may feel,
She'd need to have his breast of steel:
For has suspicion round her hovered,
While she believed herself secure—
Should she be watched, surprised, discovered,
Just as success might promise sure—
What then, alas! her life-long doom!
O! happier at once the tomb!
But vainly apprehensions rise,
In every shape, in every guise:
For such an object she can brave
Those more than terrors of the grave.

Walks to and fro the sentinel,

And soldiers from the guard-room stroll,

And round its portal sit and loll,

And many an idle tale they tell,

And jest and laugh, and rail and quaff,

Like demons at the gate of hell:

For not of this fair region they,

But from the land of William Tell,

Where first broke Freedom from her shell,

Attracted by a tyrant's pay,

They've come to make this realm a prey,

And, as a courtesan her charms,

Barter their valour and their arms.

'Tis vesper hour and from each tower,

And priory and convent dome,

The solemn bell, through street and cell,

Bids all who hear to worship come.

But Lilla turns not on her way

The pleading summons to obey:

Her glance indeed to Heaven has risen,

.But settles quickly on the prison.

In other guise to pass the guard,

By insult might the way be barred,

But, in a habit sacred dressed,

She but invoked a muttered jest;

.And, carried this first peril o'er,

Approached the subdivided door.

Here looking forth, a warder stood,

One of the callous turnkey brood,

As a rank spider, in its lair,

Keeps watch until it can ensnare,

And so his covert glance stole round,

For aught of prey that might be found.

"A prisoner is sinking here,

And soon will leave this mortal sphere;

I pray you, by our Saviour dear"—

And she impressed on brow and breast,

Redemption's holy sign—

"His spirit suffer me to cheer

　With messages divine,

Which, in the thoughts that inward spring,

Hither Madonna bids me bring."

"A dog there is by fever smote,

Who'll cheat the hangman of his throat,

And, ere from gaol to limbo driven,

By priest or monk would fain be shriven;

But all such help methinks is past,

For every breath may be his last "—

Then sprang the tears to Lilla's eyes,

But she bethought of her disguise;

And knowing pity ne'er could melt

A breast that ne'er had pity felt,

She sought to penetrate by fears

The rock insoluble by tears.

" I come by inspiration sent "—

Such was the sanction Nature lent—

" The holy offices to give,

And show the dying how to live:

As you would feel in life's last hour

This soul-invigorating power,

And many be your sins, or few,

Through all their web salvation view,

Beholding Peter open wide

The portal of the mansions blest,

Ope now this door, and be my guide

To execute his high behest:

For if through you this soul be lost—

Beware!—your own will be the cost!"

And, by her holy mission fired,

She looked indeed like one inspired,

Her air, her eye, her glowing cheek

Seemed with authority to speak,

And straight the warder stood aside,

And threw the grated portal wide;

As if he felt this act of grace

Would a whole life of guilt erase.

And she has passed the threshold dread,

That, with one stride, seems to divide

The living from the hive of dead!

Ah! would that Dante's deathless lyre

This new Inferno could portray:

And paint its depths in words of fire,

To shame and horrify the day!

Yet not unknown, nor undeclared,

Through walls and warders they have glared;

And fell it to a Saxon pen,

To bear their frightfulness to men.

'Twas Gladstone who, with giant might,

First dragged them forth in Europe's sight,

And senates, nations made to ring

With his rebuke of an evil king.

Through gate and grate and plated door,

Each locked behind ere ope'd before,

With horrid clank of bolt and key,

Unhinging brain and heart and knee,

And stifling more by sudden fear

Than by the stagnant atmosphere,

So that one gasped for breath in vain,

Finding the air itself a chain,

They moved along, the warder first,

And Lilla swiftly as she durst.

Sconced lamps a lurid glimmer cast,

Like light benighted, as they passed,

While came, from all the prison's bounds,

A chorus of discordant sounds,

And Lilla, awe-struck, closed her eyes,

As if she could shut out the cries,

And from this gulf of woe and sin,

Take refuge her own soul within.

In haste she crossed her troubled breast,

That scarce knew guilt when manifest,

For in its depths there was enshrined

That amulet, a holy mind.

At length, instinctively they halt

Before the mouth of a grim vault,

That, like a crater, dimly shows

An awful glimpse of Nature's throes,—

Not in the dread volcano's flame,

But working in the human frame,

Enough packed in those limits narrow

A realm, a startled world, to harrow!

And as, through grated aperture,

There falls by stealth a light obscure,

By Lilla's eye a space is seen,

And forms, like shadows, loom between.

But, trained to pierce the dungeon's night,

Bondage possesses quicker sight,

And from the first, she was espied,

Her figure, face, and garb descried:

And jeers were heard, and laughter wild.

Some blessed, some cursed, and some reviled,

Others in real frenzy raved,

And cried one hollow voice " *I'm saved!* "

Who were the martyrs in this hold

The eloquence of silence told :

They stood amid the noisy crowd

Wrapped in themselves, as in a shroud,

Nor seemed to know what passed around,

Though hand to hand with felons bound:

For virtue could a king invent

Such diabolic punishment!

O! more ennobling are his bonds,

Their links more honourable far,

Than are the priceless diamonds

That sparkle in his brightest star!

A few had from the trial shrunk,

And on the earth inertly sunk,

Where, pinioned to an iron rod,

They were a living cry to GOD,

That surely would through Heaven resound,

Like blood of Abel from the ground.

Others were fastened to the wall,

While heavy gyves their limbs enthral,

And matted hair and draggling beard,

Faces unwashed, and eyes all bleared,

Show plainly, as a written scroll,

How has the iron pierced the soul.

A thousand stenches mingled rise,

The walls, the air, are thick with flies,

And on the ground crawl noisome things, ·

All that disease, and foulness brings.

Is this a picture wrought with pain

In the depth of a morbid brain?

A dream by Fever's touch unfurled,

The monstrous nightmare of a world?

Alas! in such a den—as vile

As e'er was closed on blackest guile,

Two citizens of England's soil,

Her sons, though they were sons of toil,

Without transgressing to excite,

Were left to feel a tyrant's spite,

Till, crushed by the impression sad,

One turned suicide, and one went mad.

And now a swimming sense of pain

Caught, like a whirlpool, Lilla's brain,

And as it seemed to sweep her round,

And lift her reeling from the ground,

Became each object, in the gloom,

An eddy of this Maelstroom,

But like a swimmer sinking fast,

Who makes an effort as his last,

She summoned all her strength to aid,

And her o'erwhelming dread allayed.

"Where is the man who would be shriven?"

The warder, with mock fervour, said:

"By all the saints he's cheated Heaven!"

And Lilla to the spot he led.

"O! Jesu! be his sins forgiven!"

Cried Lilla, bending low her head—

For now his manacles were riven,

The ransomed prisoner was dead!

At hand another sick man lies,

Who suddenly has raised his eyes,

As if, when Lilla softly spoke,

By the archangel's trump awoke,

And, from the border of the tomb,

Brought back to life's severer gloom.

And though her eye but looked askance,

She felt—she met, his feeble glance,

For, as magnetic pulses dart,

It flashed direct upon her heart,

And she divined, before she saw,

Who lay upon that littered straw.

Her deep emotion to conceal,

She turned beside his bed to kneel,

And seeing what his look expressed,

That fear for her convulsed his breast,

So much her tenderness restrained,

That to her garb it well pertained,

And Mercy's livery in view,

Her every gesture bore its hue:

So from a distance we behold

In village spire a Saviour's fold,

Though, mantled by its ivy screen,

The spire itself may scarce be seen.

She gently raised his throbbing head,

And gleaned a pillow from his bed,

The straggling locks put from his brow,

More sensitive and shrinking now:

Then took his hand of skin and bone,

That looked like Death's within her own,

And as she clasped it, in despair,

Murmured a low, abstracted prayer,

Unconscious of the ribald jeers,

That reached her father's duller ears,

Nor able in her trance to see

Some reverently bent the knee.

But in affliction's wildest flow,

The heart will still its instincts show,

And now her father's glances dim

Made her forget herself in him:

For so mysterious the chain,

When heart is bound to heart in pain,

The conflict raging in his breast,

Left, for a space, her own at rest—

As here the hurricane has passed,

While there still sweeps its mighty blast.

He knew what impulse brought her there,

And all its tenderness could share;

But though he'd yearned to see her face,

And fold her in one last embrace,

Yet, from the perils round her spread,

The consolation turned to dread,

And this he could but faintly tell

In the one murmured word—"farewell!"

The scene all struck upon her eye,

Like the impression of a die,

As at the chink, with iron barred,

The visored light stood like a guard,

Glanced at each object as a shade

Cast deep within a forest glade,

And throwing up its sombre hue,

As in a stereoscopic view.

The roof that let rank moisture fall,

The captives fastened to the wall,

Like figures in old Egypt's caves,[3]

Or friars niched in standing graves,[4]

Each felon and his guileless mate,

United by a tyrant's hate,

The men knit to the iron rod,

Whose lives were one appeal to GOD,

Her dying father and the dead

Both lying on one littered bed,

The flies that swarmed the poisoned air,

That scarce their heavy wings could bear,

The noisome things upon the ground—

All floated in one vision round!

She staggered from this human slough

Bewildered, lost, she knew not how,

Nor heard the malefactors shout

In mockery, as she passed out;

But, quick as lightning, a wild thought

The scene again before her brought,

And, in her father's parting look,

With such hysteric impulse shook,

That, shrieking, as upon a rack,

She started round to hurry back.

Too late, alas! for, ere she turned,

A man in front her face discerned,

And as the warder seized her hand,

Her frantic purpose to withstand,

The other—Branti—for 'twas he—

Sprang forward with demoniac glee,

Held up the light, and all disguise

Rent, like a mist, before his eyes.

"Aha! methinks I know that face!

Well met, fair mistress, in this place!

What plot, I pray, against the king

Is, in your visit, on the wing?

The bird that would its end presage

We'll keep to warble in this cage.

But no! that cross, your garb, attest

The convent's cell will suit you best:

Such fitting home we'll soon provide,

And you shall be the Church's bride!"

"Your worst is done: I meet it now—

Nor life would ask from such as thou!"

Yet as she spoke, in wild alarm,

She clasped the sullen warder's arm,

As if his flinty breast would yield

The poor defence of such a shield—

"O! hide me from this dreadful man,

If your profoundest dungeon can:

Keep him by darkness from my sight,

And I will gladly sink from light."

The gaoler answered with a scoff,

To turn his chief's displeasure off,

But Branti, stung by her disdain,

His rage, his spite, could not restrain:

"Ere you again behold the day,

To see my face you'll humbly pray:

Hence—drag her to a cell—away!"

Little of need to force her on,

When she so panted to be gone,

And to the gaoler felt so light

She seemed in sooth a bird in flight.

And not without a secret sway

Her hand in his a moment lay:

As friction snatches fire from wood,

Her touch e'en here awakened good,

And when he thrust her in the cell,

A spark of pity from him fell,

Though, as base metal rings perverse,

His pity stumbled in a curse.

She heard him not, nor knew he spoke,

No sound through her abstraction broke,

And to the darkness she was blind,

A deeper night was in her mind;

Yet a perception of relief,

As 'twere a star, peered through her grief,

She thought not, dreamt not, whence it ca

But Branti's absence gave the gleam;

And now, as on a mirror cast,

It showed the terrors she had past,

And she felt borne, as by a wave,

Into the refuge of this grave.

But when—too soon—she was immured,

And when she heard the door secured,

The bolts seemed through her side to dart,

As if their socket were her heart;

And now she could not check a cry,

And prostrate sank, as if to die,

Then, in her frenzy, turned to fly:

Alas! 'twas but to meet the door,

And fall its iron foot before.

From this distraction to reclaim,

With thought on thought, Composure came,

As imperceptibly the dew,

That, in its fall, eludes our view,

And she grew patient and resigned,

As if the night had left her mind,

Or burst the clouds that hid its sky,

And showed her Heaven still on high.

But 'tis by love divine foreshown,

We are not made to be alone:

If there be no vibration lent,

What music in the instrument!

  nd should it long unswept remain,

Then discord mingles with its strain :·

So with our faculties repressed—

They fall to ruin in the breast,

And, where was harmony complete,

Soon Reason totters on her seat.

And silently this blight fell round

As Lilla lay upon the ground:

And every moment, every hour,

Increased the pressure of its power:

For though her father's image oft

Would raise emotions deep and soft,

And for a time bear her above

Her terrors in her filial love,

Still came the thought she was alone,

In this deep sepulchre of stone,

And, through the watches of the night,

It grew in horror and in might,

Until it made her narrow cell

Its battlemented citadel.

And so Time loitered slowly on

Leaning his idle scythe upon,

For nothing could he find to mow

Where every thought would blighted grow,

And, where the hour-glass was the brain,

His steps, the minutes, fell with pain,

And trod into the living clock,

As drops of water dint the rock.

Came no distinctive shade to say

Or when 'twas night or when 'twas day;

No voice, no sound, but Nature dumb

Echoed at times a distant hum,

Such as might spring from memories dear

Responding to the listening ear,

Just as, when pressed, the captive shell

Resounds the waves it loves so well.

No visitor her dungeon sought,

A hand unseen provisions brought,

Which through a panel of the door

A box turned on a pivot bore,

And, grazing on the iron bar,

This was her only calendar.

At last they ope'd the dungeon door,

A lamp advancing to explore,

Though to her eyes its lurid rays

Seemed to present the sun's full blaze.

The sullen warder entered then,

And followed quick two other men,

Who, by the flashing of their arms,

Were seen at once to be gendarmes.

"Up now, haste!" the warder cried,

"You're bound upon a pleasant ride,

A carriage waits you in the yard,

These gentlemen will be your guard.

To a sweet home they bear you hence—

The convent of Black Penitents."

Her cruel sentence Lilla heard,

Without a gesture or a word;

And, though her knees would scarce support,

Passed with her keepers to the court.

THE CONVENT.

If e'er you'd see Religion marred,

Let it be ranked with punishments,

And render it a bondage hard,

As in that Sisterhood ill-starred,

The order of Black Penitents.

Their convent hangs upon a height,

   As if it there had flown,

Arrested in its heavenward flight,

And driven weary to alight,

   By its dead weight of stone,

That, like a frame of mortal birth,

Chained down its hundred souls to earth.

Around there rose a lofty wall,

And peered above two towers tall,

That o'er the country threw a scowl,

As friars glance from 'neath a cowl:

A narrow court the walls invest,

As 'twere the convent's sullen breast,

Where shut within itself, it gives

No thought to all that outward lives:

And, still beyond, a wall sweeps round,

The cemetery's awful bound—

So circumscribed each Sister's doom

She steps from prison to the tomb!

But who would give that holy name—

Sister—where the term would shame,

For here the object was to part,

Not to draw nearer, heart and heart,

And pure and sullied to confound

In one promiscuous gulf profound.

The fair without and foul within,

Poor frailty, and leprous sin,

The faithless wife, the spotted maid,

The wronged, the perjured, the betrayed—

All compassed by one stern decree

Made up the hapless company.

No Sister's loving fellowship

Where locked each breast and sealed each lip,

And Nature's soft emotions all

By cruel vows were held in thrall.

How sisters! when within her veil,

Each nun inclosed her spirit's pale,

And, in this narrow confine furled,

Saw in herself her only world!

And yet, withal, as Sisters, too,

They might appear to outward view

Albeit not in earthly hue—

For when, at call of midnight bell,

They sally from their lonely cell,

And, through the chapel dimly lit,

To their appointed places flit—

As in long file they bend the knee—

They seem a band of ghosts to be.

Sat in an oratory old

The Abbess of this convict fold,

An image of its canons stern:

Her face, inanimate and cold,

But of a lifeless sorrow told,

As 'twere a monumental urn,

That 'neath its dismal shadow gave

The soul, in its own breast, a grave.

All human feeling she ignored,

For what was human she abhorred,

'Twas weakness, folly, error, sin,

The taint original within.

Nor licence for herself she sought,

But daily practised what she taught,

And pushed for Heaven's far retreat

With weighted heart and shackled feet,

Not raising up her torpid soul

To share the race and win the goal.

With low obeisance came a Nun,

Her eyes cast down that gaze to shun,

As fearing might some trace be seen,

That once a woman she had been,

" Reverend mother, at our gates,

An escort with a sinner waits,

This rescript, through the grating caught,

Shows whence and wherefore she is brought."

The sealed despatch the Abbess took

With an awakened, kindling look—

For if a point where she could feel,

It was the bosom of her zeal.

Adown the scroll she cast her eye—

" A traitress—intrigante—and spy!

O! what an evil legion here

O'er one poor soul to domineer,

And plunge into a depth of sin,

From hatred of all discipline.

How blest my lot that I shall be

An instrument to set her free,

And, with my withered, palsied hand,

Snatch from the burning one more brand!

But bring her, as our rules provide,

First to salute me as her guide."

Her hands upon her bosom pressed,

And bending low at this behest,

The Nun in silence took her way

The stern injunction to obey;

And, though the moments were but few,

The Abbess in her fervour grew,

As covertly the Nun discerned,

When soon with Lilla she returned.

Not with misgiving, or in fear,

Came Lilla, though a captive, here,

For, if not liberty to roam,

The convent would afford a home,

Where, if Religion bore a rod,

'Twas but to raise the soul to God,

While from her dungeon to the light

Was to escape to morn from night.

And this impression, glad but chaste,.

Her spirit and her look embraced,

And like her garb portrayed an aim

A Sister of Mercy well became.

As mariners at sea explore

The outlines of a rising shore,

The Abbess scrutinized her face,

As there her character to trace;

And in the haven of her soul,

Saw rocks arise, and billows roll;

For to her mind, by zeal distorted,

Where hope looked forth, there guilt resorted.

"You wear the clothing of the lamb,

But the fierce wolf breaks through the sham,

And could a robe your nature show,

A blushing scarlet it would glow,

Away! prepare by vigils stern—

Remorse that racks, and thoughts that burn—

Our order's vestiture to earn!

And when for every sin you bleed

You'll come to Christ a lamb indeed."

Quailed Lilla at this sharp reproof

As 'neath the rushing charger's hoof

The wounded, who still cling to life,

Recoil amid the battle's strife:

But everything around her here

She had been tutored to revere,

And whatsoe'er the Church might say,

She knew to hear was to obey,

So, meekly her obeisance done,

She followed forth the silent Nun.

Across a court their steps they bent,

And down a cloistered passage went,

But not a word was interchanged,

As through the dreary pile they ranged.

Like the blank cover of a book

Is that Black Sister's curtained look:

Ah! could we raise it up and read,

The tale might make the sternest bleed.

Within the convent church they stood;

They knelt before the holy rood;

And ere she raised her glance again,

Lilla had lost her chamberlain.

As from a landscape fades a hue

Clouds sombre in their passage threw,

Leaving no trace where it had been.

She stole away unheard, unseen:

And now unwatched, all silent round,

A sanctuary Lilla found,

And nestled to this place of rest

As were its floor her mother's breast.

And did her vision not delude

Not hers alone this chastened mood,

For at Madonna's blessed shrine,

Where stood her effigy divine,

O'er human sins and sorrows weeping—

There, on the step, a nun was sleeping.

Solemn and still the vaulted aisles,

And in the midst the dismal nave,

That loomed up through their grim defiles

Less like a temple than a cave—

For, low and broad, the columns all

Seemed hewn complete from mountain wall,

And neither strength nor lightness gave,

And no relief of architrave,

But 'neath the roof seemed bedding down,

Just like a despot 'neath his crown,

And knit above in Gothic curve,

That now the eye could not observe,

Might represent a despot's frown.

And there the Nun was lyiug down,

Stretched at Madonna's holy feet,

Her sleep so tranquil and so sweet!

The tears the sculptor sought to trace

On that benign, seraphic face,

The tears the Dolorosa shed—

Fell they upon her marble bed,

Surely the Nun had raised her head!

Strained Lilla's gaze if it could mark

In such repose the vital spark,

But too profound the sleeper's rest,

Too like her pillow was her breast;

And glided Lilla to the spot

As though she fain would share her lot,

Yet half in doubt, and half in dread—

For she surmised the Nun was dead.

Laid out before the Virgin weeping,

As though in truth she were but sleeping—

In all her daily garb arrayed,

And down her breast a cross of white,

With hands clasped o'er, as if she prayed,

Reposing, in Faith's conscious might,

Upon that rock, that emblem bright!

Her votive ring was on her finger,

And in her face a gleam of light,

As though her spirit still might linger,

Or—ere it took its upward flight—

Had left this impress exquisite.

Such the inscription, meek and faint,

Oft traced upon a dungeon wall,

Nor plea, nor protest, nor complaint,

But in its silence blending all—

The story of a hapless thrall!

And here, much sooner to decay,

'Twas writ upon a wall of clay,

That, fit to domicile a queen,

A prison—dungeon—yet had been,

Perverted from its mission high

That she 'twas meant to beautify,

A corpse might live, a saint might die!

Through the deep windows, dwarfed and small,

Night's warning shadows 'gan to fall,

Partaking of the ghostly stains,

That dyed and blurred the mullioned panes—

As intermixed and undefined,

The images in Lilla's mind:

To her how welcome were the veil

Within the Church's real pale,

F

For there—distracted, lost—she'd find

A refuge safe and usage kind.

But now what ministering voice

To smoothe the way and lead her choice!

What hand to guide her halting feet,

And bring her to the blest retreat!

No solemn tones from organ peal,

No loving nuns around her kneel,

One only aim—to chill and awe—

In all she heard and all she saw.

The Church, too tender to reject,

Yet named her not a bride elect,

But took her from the state a slave

To train and tutor for the grave.

How different, how happy she,

Advancing to the altar free,

And feeling that her hand was given

Unshackled to the King of Heaven!

Slowly the gloom with shade on shade,

The darker touch of night displayed,

Till, blending in one hue profound,

It settled like a cloud around.

But a subdued effulgence soon

Proclaimed the advent of the moon:

It fell the window near upon,

And through its varied colours shone,

Showing a form, a woman fair,

Her eyes bedewed, cast down her hair,

And kneeling at the Saviour's feet,

A picture—O, divinely sweet!

For ne'er could Mercy's voice declare

A reconcilement more complete.

Gazed Lilla, with a look serene,

On the bewailing Magdalene,

Until the face so long in view

From her an animation drew.

And, 'lumined by the moonbeams soft,

The eyes rose hopefully aloft,

Emotion lit the kindling cheek,

The lips, unlocking, seemed to speak—

No marvel that she bent the knee

A miracle so strange to see!

But suddenly the vision changed,

Like summer night by tempest ranged,

The figure that on wings of love

Had borne her thoughts the earth above,

Now from the window seemed to rise

With aspect fierce and wrathful eyes:

Then, towering up, sublimely tall,

A shadow on the chapel wall,

Onward in fell swoop it pressed—

She felt its hand upon her breast:

It froze her blood, it stayed her breath,

A form of horror and of death.

O! let the arm uplifted smite,

If 'twould deliver from this sight:

But now around vibrates a sound

All evil spirits will confound;

For none dare meet those tones that swell,

Like dirges, from the convent bell.

And was it all a horrid dream?

And had she there sunk down in sleep?

Full softly did the moonlight beam,

And lit the window with its gleam,

But still she felt a tremor creep—

A current in her bosom deep:

For now she heard distinct a bell

Tolling a funereal knell,

And there a form, in black arrayed,

Clóse at her side, a shadow, stayed.

Then, like a meteor's weird flame,

A horrid thought upon her came,

A thought in keeping with her mood—

That the dead Nun beside her stood.

And shuddering, through all her frame,

She sank before the holy rood,

And low pronounced the blessed name

That angels evermore acclaim!

But one look at Madonna's shrine

Showed, 'neath the effigy divine,

The corpse, all hushed, still on its bed—

Upward its partner soul had fled,

And, rescued from its bonds of clay,

Never again that form would wed,

Until the awful Judgment Day.

The figure standing at her side,

Was—soon she saw—her recent guide;

And though uplifted was her hand,

'Twas but attention to command;

And on her lip a finger laid,

Admonishing the trembling maid,

Repressed the cry that half arose,

Convulsive as a nightmare's throes.

"Silence, and follow!" she softly said;

And quick the way to a postern led;

While Lilla, still as in a dream,

That round her denser mazes spread,

Swift as the moonlight's darting gleam,

Forth from the silent chancel sped,

Yet ere they pass the threshold dread

That stands the boundary extreme,

Atween the living and the dead,

They both a Paternoster say,

And for the souls departed pray,

Then, as an amulet they'd found,

Advance into the holy ground.

No sculptured stone or moss-grown mound,

But only quarried pits were there,'

And bones, all whitened, lay around

And trunkless skulls, as bleached and bare,

Like remnants of a vampire's fare!

Alas! to think they e'er had been,

The temples of a living soul—

Those vacant sockets once had seen

And glistened with a light serene,

And from their orbs love's glances stole,

Illumining the glowing cheek,

Where beauty's blush had seemed to speak,

And there, as on a coin of gold,

Impressed in Nature's faultless mould,

The hand divine its stamp had given,

The image of the King of Heaven.

Here what rich spoils grim Death had won!

"O! vanity!" exclaimed the Nun.

" Who would the world's delights prefer,

To works that might by Faith be done,

Would not this sight, these bones, deter,

When such the course that all must run?

Ah! were those works, that mission, mine,

All other objects could I shun!

But rules our sisterhood confine,

We may do nothing but repine!

To-night another mortal's clay

Another lifeless, soulless thing,

With dirge and taper here we' bring;

And when to live is death each day

Can you our canons stern obey?—

Stranger—maiden—sister, say!"

She paused—a pause might be a sigh,

Unheard, except it were on high,

And then again her voice arose,

In the same accents of repose—

"If not—if you distrust your heart—

You may, are you but bold, depart!"

Sank Lilla weeping at her feet—

"O! save me, save!" she whispered low.

Then spoke the Nun with cadence sweet—

"If you the jeopardy will meet—

And 'tis far greater than you know—

I, from this spot, a way can show,

And though the peril be obscure,

Better to dare than to endure,

For 'tis a dreadful thing to be

So doomed and life-enthralled as we.

And if, before my vows had bound

A path from this retreat I'd found,

Wer't torment, death, the stake to face—

The risk I'd shrunk not to embrace!"

And for an instant's space she stood,

As launched upon dark Memory's flood,

And by its billows, strong though mute,

Tossed in an agony acute:

Nor Lilla's voice the silence broke,

Responsive to the words she spoke,

For though gave sympathy a key

That might unlock her reverie,

And few the moments that remain

For her to break or weld her chain,

She, thinking of the Nun alone,

In *her* despair forgot her own.

Tolled quicker now the solemn knell,

And o'er that flood of memories fell,

Admonishing the Nun's rapt ear,

As warned of yore the sea-cliff bell*

Through mingled mist and darkness drear,

That danger, though unseen, was near.

"Sister, those sounds, sad mentors, tell

Soon minutes to a life-time swell:

No longer we must linger here.

Without yon postern, in the wall,

A priest awaits our mother's call:

For only at the open grave,

We claim such blessed help to save,

So rigid is our code to keep

Man's foot without the convent's sweep.

Are you resolved and do you choose

Your bonds to rivet or to loose?"

"O! holy Sister! wer't to die,

I'd still decide and pray to fly!

Your help and your sweet blessing give,

And, by God's help, I yet shall live."

" May angels on your footsteps tend!

Blest Mary her assistance lend!

Now mark!—for this the minute's brink

When you must boldly leap or sink—

While at the grave the Padre prays,

A portress at the postern stays:

You'll see her once in worship kneel,

That moment you must outward steal,

And fly—'tis onward—to the coast,

One step to falter, you are lost,

For o'er the country, far and near,

Our bell will the alarum spread,

And trumpet in each startled ear—

A convict—such we are—has fled!

Now, stand within this shaded nook,

The door 's unbarred—it opens—look!"

A Nun before the postern stood,

The guard of the Black Sisterhood:

Enveloped in her sable suit,

A votive and perpetual mute,

No meeter could, I ween, be.found

As warder of a burial-ground.

The door, though open, she held fast,

As fearing prowlers might rush past,

And scarce inclined her head the least

Before the blessing of the Priest.

Turned Lilla to address her guide,

But she had softly left her side,

For now from the adjacent fane

Came slowly on a mournful train,

With tapers lit and raised on high,

And chanting—awful lullaby—

The requiem's exalted strain

To ears that ne'er shall hear again.

Close, closer round the bier they throng,

And louder there intone the song,

As though they'd have their sister know

Who love, who mourn, who guard her so;

Believing as they round her wait

Their dirge will reach far Heaven's gate;

For, though the gulf be wide between,

Bright angels float above unseen,

And, borne that brazen cross before,

The soul now launched shall gain the shore.

The censer swings and incense springs

In homage to the King of Kings;

And the stoled Priest, with holy water,

Sprinkles the Church's wedded daughter,

As onward, like a train of state,

They bear her to the narrow gate,

Whence prayers shall wing her on with speed,

Though Purgatory's fires impede,

For they are taught their penance here

Shall bridge for them that chasm drear.

There was a ministering awe

In everything she heard and saw,

That Lilla's soul might well impress

With a religious tenderness;

And gazing with impassioned eye,

She half determined not to fly,

Bewildered by that strange amaze

As by a spiritual haze,

That, like a mirage, gave to view

Each object in illusion's hue,

And all a different aspect wore,

From what it was, or seemed before:

The convent's crushing discipline

Now but a holy war with sin;

And who would shrink from such a strife,

Its end—when won—eternal life!

But this impression, though it fell,

Was but a momentary spell;

For as the mirage's display,

Its streams and meads, all melts away,

So from her mind these fancies fled,

And, in their place, the desert spread.

All but too late the warning came

Her shaken purpose to reclaim,

But it awoke a courage high,

Resolved to still succeed or die.

Forth from the shadow of the wall

Where, clear and full, the moonbeams fall,

She glides, she stands, before them all,

While dust into the grave they toss

Raising aloft the holy cross,

For by its elevation free,

Death's swallowed up in victory,

And at its jubilant display

The watchful portress kneels to pray.

Not pausing to discover more,

Lilla flew to the postern door,

·She seized the latch, it would not rise—

Again with all her strength she tries,

And, now the secret she has found,

The door flies open with a bound.

Not need to urge that cry behind,

She rushes onward like the wind,

On—breathless on, nor looks to see

Who may her swift pursuer be.

On, on, still on, o'er rock and steep,

Where boldest hunter ne'er would sweep.

And far around is heard the swell,

The loud alarm—of the convent bell.

THE SILENT PASSION.

'Twas on a lonely mountain track

That Lilla, pausing, first looked back,

But shadows indistinctness threw

O'er every object brought to view,

And vainly down the path she glanced—

Who there could see if foes advanced?

Whate'er of peril might be nigh,

No more, no further could she fly,

'Twas here to yield, or sinking, die—

For panting, heaving, with each breath,

She wrestled, as it seemed, with death:

And yet the lightest, faintest sound

Made her rise drooping from the ground,

As, rather than her fate embrace,

She still would perish in the chase;

And, even when too clear the end,

Still with her latest breath contend.

Sterile the scene, and lone and wild,

With rocks around, like ramparts, piled:

Here, scarped, they formed a bastion brave,

Here sloping back, a glacis gave,

Here were o'erthrown as by a wave!

And ran the rough-hewn road atween,

Where once a torrent-bed had been:

Not art the granite way had made,[7]

That pavement the volcano laid.

The stars were waning in the sky

As rose her mournful glance on high,

And in the East, that point divine, :

Of Christian, Jew, and Turk the shrine,

A sheet of purple hue and red,

Like a rich altar-cloth, was spread,

As if the sun, before he came,

Offered to God his waking flame,

Then, crowned, arose with royal sway,

The consecrated King of day.

How sweet the morning's balmy air,

That circled all the mountain bare,

G

Whereon nor wood nor herbage grew,

To catch the breeze, or sip the dew.

And everywhere 'twas silent round,

Not the faint vestige of a sound—

No soaring lark, with tuneful song,

As I have heard in England's isle,

When through the night I've roved along,

And caught the morning's first sweet smile :

No bleating lambs, no lowing kine,

Nor e'en the watch-dog's mournful whine—

Nothing to cheer or to beguile

Throughout the dreary lone defile.

Yet Lilla strained her timid ear,

Too conscious peril must be near,

And that the day, to others light,

Would haply bring to her a blight—

O! darker than the darkest night!

Clearer and wider o'er the sky,

Each moment the swift sunbeams fly,

And, with the pageantry of morn,

The whole of the broad East adorn.

The purple altar-cloth and red

Is now a thousand banners spread,

Which, blazoned o'er with shining gold,

Exceeding royalty unfold,

And trooping up, and sweeping round,

The car of day with pomp surround,

Till comes the Sun, the monarch bright,

In all the majesty of light.

Still Lilla crouched where she had fell,

Alike to move or stay afraid,

While weariness and hunger preyed

G 2

As in a leaguered citadel,

Defended gallantly and well,

On that slight frame, that now so weak,

Drooped like the roses in her. cheek.

Safety this lonely spot might give

To the despairing fugitive,

But here to stay were soon to feel

From want more pangs than death could deal,

And did she seek the haunts of men,

Disgrace and bondage met her then.

Not long could she distracted muse,

Necessity compelled to choose;

For now the breeze, though faint and low,

Brought up spent voices from below—

Like shot from an approaching foe;

And from a crag, which stood out bold,

The watch-tower of that mountain hold,

She saw ascending up the track

A band despatched to bring her back,

For as the Padre led them on,

Their purpose was too clearly shown,

And a mixed throng, a score at least,

Attended on the eager priest.

Gathering her strength as 'twere a train,

That might her cumbered limbs restrain,

She onward fled, she knew not where,

But in the mountains to remain,

Among its crags and passes bare,

Her only chance of safety there—

For, swept around, the open plain

Were but the convent's gates again.

Now reached the mountain's lofty head,

She stands as on an eyry high,

Betwixt the land, the sea, the sky,

Which here on every side are spread,

A prospect beautiful, if dread.

But her keen gaze is on the sea,

Whose waves, in their unbroken flow,

The vaulted sphere reflected show,

As calm, as silent, and as free,

A second sky it seems to be,

And there were birds careering too,

With wings of white they skimmed the blue,

A dozen gallant sail and more

That might be reckoned from the shore—

From that high peak, that rose so grand,

As 'twere the bulwark of the land!

The sea like a wide gulf, before,

And far beneath the golden strand,

Encircling with a zone of sand,

Which wildest waves might not pass o'er;

There seemed, where'er she looked, a bound,

Through which no outlet might be found.

Ah! would yon bark that came so nigh,

Cleaving the waters with its keel,

As if it were a plough of steel,

Attend her supplicating cry,

Her wild, her desperate appeal!

The crew, so 'minished to her eye,

Could they so far behold her kneel,

And see her wave her kerchief high

In her distracted agony!

What meant the streamer hauled up now,

A signal from the mast displayed?

Had Mary Mother heard the vow

Her soul in its distress had made?

Yes! yes! 'twas on the flag portrayed—

A cross of red, traced clear and bright,

Upon a field of spotless white!

Well may that flag her eye delight,

For 'tis the banner of the free,

That rules with sovereignty the sea,

And though behind the foe 's in sight,

It nerves her to resume her flight,

As it cheers Britons to the fight,

Where'er, by England's high decree,

In honour's vanguard it may be.

A dark ravine winds steeply down,

Round jutting rock and plateau brown,

And Lilla plunges in the maze,

With eager foot, though shuddering gaze,

For, scanned through all its depths from this,

It seems a bottomless abyss.

Not many steps can she advance

Before a chasm arrests her glance,

But quickened by a yell behind,

That rushed upon her like the wind,

She saw not lurking Death before,

And, with one bound, she vaulted o'er,

Alighting, as an antelope,

On an abrupt and rugged slope,

And sliding down the granite hill,

Like a swift impetuous rill.

A fearful sight to see her leap,

Where scarce a goat would dare to creep,

Now reeling back upon a crag,

Now springing forward like the stag,

Insensible that, from the height,

Her fierce pursuers watched her flight.

And only seeing on before,

A boat was pushing for the shore.

From 'midst a cloud of smoke and flame,

Down the ravine a volley came,

And cave and mount, on every side,

With a combined salute replied,

As 'twere the rolling thunder crash

Following the lightning's vivid flash,

And high above there rose a shout,

A thousand echoes rang about;

For, as the bullets through the air

A path with hissing fury tear,

Winged on an errand past recall,

The fugitive is seen to fall!

A peasant, who had led the way,

Leaps quickly down to seize the prey,

While sbirri and gendarmes behind,

More slowly round the gully wind;

But she has heard their coming feet,

And rises with a step more fleet,

For 'twas not Death's, but Terror's dart,

That had transfixed her bursting heart;

And, once recovered from the shock,

She glides again from rock to rock,

And, with one effort made to reach,

Sinks breathless, senseless, on the beach.

From out the boat the steersman sprung,

A man of noble mien and young,

And one impatient, rapid stride,

Brought him to the maiden's side.   ·

Her face, her form, her sacred dress,

Her flight, and her unconsciousness,

With the pursuing gang behind,

A moment's doubt threw o'er his mind.

'Twas plain some mystery was here—

Could he, a stranger, interfere?

But he recalled her signal made,

As, kneeling, she invoked his aid,

The volley fired, with deadly aim,

As down the rugged steeps she came;

And now before him, in full cry,

He saw her enemies draw nigh:

He scanned her youthful, pallid face,

And not a shade of guilt could trace,

But plainly, though no blush of youth,

The spiritual hues of truth—

Presented, with vraisemblance rare,

Sweet innocence, a portrait, there.

And, last, what needs must win the brave,

A woman claimed his arm to save,

And, while seemed fate and life to pause,

To his decision left her cause.

As might a parent some fond child,

He gently raised her from the ground,

Regardless of the din around,

And the gesticulations wild,

The menaces that loud resound,

As her pursuers downward bound:

And swift he bears her to the boat,

"Give way! give way!"—they are afloat:

Again there is a volley's crash,

The bullets in the water splash,

But only by their range to show

They're 'yond the malice of their foe:

And o'er the sea's calm breast they glide,

Just like a ripple of its tide.

Restored by the inspiring air,

Her senses came to Lilla there,

Each with a music in its voice,

That bids her, looking round, rejoice,

But ere her feeble lips can speak

The joy enlightening her cheek,

They reach the yacht, that, like a swan,

Floats gracefully the waves upon,

A rope is thrown, the boat hauled taut,

And safely to the deck she's brought.

The steersman stood before her now,

Sole master of the gallant ship;

The light of kindness on his brow,

The smile of welcome on his lip,

A pledge of courtly fellowship!

Familiar to her eye he seemed,

Like one of whom she once had dreamed,

Yet coming back as 'mid a haze

To her bewildered, doubting gaze,

Till, lifted up the misty screen,

As by a flood of Memory's rays,

The view in all its breadth displays,

And well remembered was his mien,

With the suggestive background seen.

"A second time in utmost need,

You've come to aid me, and have freed;

And I have double thanks to give,

That then you saved—that still I live.

You have forgotten! yet I trace

A dim remembrance on your face,

I will recall the time, the place—

A summer night, Palermo gaol,

That, like a brand, still makes me quail,

Deliverer as prompt as bold,

You snatched me from a ruffian's hold—

The same who with his baneful power

Pursued me to the present hour."

Before the Englishman could speak

A crimson flush suffused his cheek—

For swifter than in words the heart

Its deep emotions will impart,

And what their nature frankly show

In their unbidden overflow.

" 'Tis well for him," he muttered low,

" That when his knife was on my breast

He stood not forth so manifest.

But, lady, cheer! and safe and free,

Forget a while such things can be;

And when your mournful tale I know

We may for ever foil your foe."

They brought her up a cup of wine,

The juice of sweet Marsala's vine;

And on the deck a table spread,

With a broad awning overhead,

Her host sat down beside her there,

The slight repast to help and share—

For he who'd know the art to please

Must by his actions place at ease.

So long oppressed her lightened breast,

Felt a delicious sense of rest,

And in the scene, the objects round,

Relief, assurance, comfort found.

Pursuit she need to dread no more,

Left far behind the rocky shore,

And where so lately men had been,

Were only fading mountains seen.

The sea, spread like a mirror fair,

Was swept by a soft floating air,

An air so light, that it might be

The breathing of the sleeping sea;

And it conveyed to Lilla's heart,

What Freedom's lips alone impart,

A sense, a consciousness of soul,

That ope'd as an unfolded scroll,

And, by a flash, her mind endued

With all the light of womanhood.

It bore her back—that witching light—

As 'twere the moon's fantastic beams,

Into a labyrinth of dreams,

That had, at times, with glimmer bright,

Beguiled captivity's dark night,

Leading her forth by woods and streams.

Nor roamed she lonely through the land,

But 'neath the cool, refreshing shade,

Acacias and tall chestnuts made,

One walked beside her, hand in hand,

And knit by some more mystic band.

His form the same in every place,

Though she could ne'er recall his face,

But, like the object of a vow,

It looked, it shone upon her now.

Not much she said, but in each word

A soft, sweet melody was heard,

As if, enkernelléd in the sound,

The gentle breath of feeling stirred,

Like the enchanted Beauty bound,

By necromantic skill profound,

Within a tree's encircling round,

And who, whene'er the breeze awoke,

Amidst the rustling foliage spoke.

But quickly as the moments fled,

And buoyant as her spirit felt,

Upborne by Love's sustaining belt,

That o'er the tide so lightly sped—

Yet failed her strength and drooped her head;

For nature, 'mid emotions deep,

Still claimed the soothing balm of sleep.

And scarcely had her looks expressed

This present, urgent need of rest,

When came the stewardess to show

A cabin for her use below:

And, to the hatch by Mowbray tended,

She gladly with her guide descended.

At last, in freedom and in peace,

A pillow, white as snow, she pressed,

The storm-tossed swimmer was at rest.

And, soft as dew upon a fleece,

Fell sleep in·silence on her breast,

Gave to her mind a full release

From all the burden that oppressed,

And not one phantom thought arose

To break the calm of her repose.

Ah, sweet restorer, healing Sleep!

Thou benefactor of our kind,

What weary vigils do we keep,

Through what a maze of thought we sweep,

When thee we seek and fail to find!

But when in thy embrace entwined,

We feel thy lulling influence creep

Alike o'er body and o'er mind,

And when thou minist'rest serene,

Like Charity, unknown, unseen,

But oft where Charity ne'er trod,

We hail thee Almoner of God!

For bringest thou to human grief

An interval of blest relief,

And, what His Hand alone can give,

The strength to bear and heart to live.

And thou'll forsake the titled lord,

Who revels at a banquet board,

Turn from a dainty bed of down,

And e'en despise a royal crown,

To come by stealth, sweet Sleep, and bless

Misery's couch with thy caress.

No sound on Lilla's slumbers broke,

And day was gone ere she awoke.

The stewardess, in waiting nigh,

Her wants was eager to supply,

But these were few; for she arose

Invigorated by repose,

Nor could a buoyant impulse check

To leave the cabin for the deck.

The stars in millions shone on high,

As 'twere a *festa* in the sky;

And every orb itself surpassed

In the illumination vast,

While the hushed deep, and 'jacent shore,

Seemed in their silence to adore.

And, moving on its canvas wing,

The yacht looked like a living thing,

A spirit skipping o'er the sea

And joining in the jubilee.

Knew Lilla by her beating heart,

The beat that rapture's pulses dart,

Before she dared to raise her eye,

That Mowbray, though unseen, was nigh,

And as she watched the dark, still tide,

He crossed the gangway to her side.

She felt the blood glow in her cheek,

And feared to trust her voice to speak,

For by the tremor in its tone,

Her innate pleasure might be shown,

And she would still that secret keep,

Still in her bosom let it sleep,

Conceal with thinnest veil the flame

That shines through every mask the same,

Beams from the eye, lights up the face,

In words and acts reveals its trace,

H

And always shows its own sweet grace:

Nor did she for the moment fail,

For yet the flame was dim and pale.

Before—the thought they soon must part

Had, like a dagger, pierced her heart,

And it had seemed to make a bound,

Under the anguish of the wound;

But that physician of the mind

Whose touch the widest gash can bind,

Who soothes that, slowly on the wheel,

We may hereafter keenlier feel,

Deluding Hope, from this fresh grief

With his elixir gave relief,

And blinded to the future night

In present transport of delight.

"This hour wields an influence blest,"

He said in that soft flowing tone

Pervades Italia's tongue alone:

"Why has it, then, infringed your rest,

When thought, like waves, should feel the calm

It sheds upon them like a charm,

And you may claim its healing might,

Fatigue's just guerdon, as a right?

In truth, I'd almost dare to chide

Only the power were denied—

For how could I find words to blame

A fault that as a favour came!"

"Such kind reproof would but declare

Your hospitality and care:

But, sir, indeed through these I've found

A calm as deep as that around:

H 2

Here I enjoy the sweet repose

The hour o'er every object throws:

So great a change surrounds my eye—

The dungeon's night for yon clear sky!

I look upon the circling sea,

It tells me silently I'm free;

I feel the air around me sweep—

O! this is rest, and this is sleep!"

" You give the hour and the expanse

The fascination of romance,

The more as your own life has lent

A tinge to the sad sentiment.

I will not ask you to recal

Scenes that, though past, must still appal,

But, what remains to vex or hurt,

I'd gladly know can I avert."

A glance from her dark beaming eyes

Her feelings told without disguise—

But she drew back from the surprise.

"O, thanks! but you've a right to know,

All your compassion would forego;

And, since your kindness can invite,

The tale is easy to recite."

She told it out, nor he once spoke,

Nor with an exclamation broke

The narrative that, like a spell,

Upon his ears, his spirit, fell,

And even when it ceased to thrill,

Awhile he seemed to listen still.

"Now by yon land before us spread,

And by great Heaven overhead,

By all your wrongs, and by man's right,

That yet shall triumph over might,

I swear, if ere there come a day,

When Italy shall stand at bay,

And throw her heavy yoke away,

Whatever fortune may betide,

This tale shall range me on her side,

And spur me, by its poignant woes,

Amidst the thickest of her foes."

"You are as generous as brave—

And not more free the sea's wild wave,

And hence you know not, nor can feel,

The terrors that beset the slave,

Who, under power's iron heel,

Is born to serve and trained to kneel.

Yet not alone our fallen state

Delays the struggle you await;

And Italy, so long oppressed,

Would soon from all her freedom wrest,

If but her rulers were the foe

She had to meet and overthrow:

But close at hand the Austrians stand,

And hirelings come from Switzerland,—

And shall we ever see the day

When she can battle such array?

Yes, yes! I bless you for the hope,

That such a happy day shall be!

I, shipwrecked, clutch it as a rope

On a tempestuous raging sea.

For, O! I feel my country's wrongs

Speak to me with a thousand tongues,

In my own hapless, cruel doom

And from my father's prison-tomb!"   .

But through her tears the moonbeams brought

To Mowbray's mind a cheering thought:

"He still may live—nay, may be free,

Enfranchised by the amnesty,

Which, from his hand by Europe wrung,

Your king has to his captives flung.

A frigate bears in bonds to Spain,

As exiles, the unhappy train,

And if you will the voyage dare,

We'll seek—may find, your father there."

If she would dare!—what peril grim

Would she not gladly dare with him!

And this—O! 'twas a draught of joy

That no misgiving could alloy.

She feared her answer might express

More than a maiden should confess,

All that her eye and cheek could show,

In their warm southern flush and glow,

Only the friendly shade of night

Obscured and masked their tell-tale light;

So her assent was but a word,

Wherein this rapture was not heard.

And for a space—one moment brief—

To be alone was a relief,

While Mowbray sought the helm amain,

To shape their course direct for Spain—

For now those transports she could still

That sent through every vein a thrill,

And place a guard upon the pleasure

Hid in her bosom like a treasure.

Not yet to part, but on the sea

With him, her champion, to be—

For day on day, a week or more,

It seemed eternity in store!

Like moonbeams on a placid lake,

Whose silent flow no ripples break,

Which seems a crystal to the eye,

Though 'neath a gulf of waters lie,

So peace its silver, mystic light

Shed o'er her face that happy night,

Nor through those beams one ripple stole

To tell what depths were in her soul.

PART THE FIFTH.

MEETING AND PARTING.

A SHIP is speeding on her way,

And near the cliffs of Spain are seen,

With swarthy face and turban green—

Like the Moors of the olden day,

Who here upheld the crescent's sway

With lances bold and laws serene:

And leeward comes another sail,

Flying before the tempered gale,

Through the saluting showers of spray,

That sparkle in the sunlight's trail,

Like gems upon a bodice gay,

As round the breasting bows they play,

While she advances through the waters,

One of the ocean's fairest daughters.

Aloft the English flag she spread,

And with an ensign flowing wide,

The gallant bark ahead replied—

An ensign on whose mingled thread

Auspicious stars their promise shed,

While glowing stripes from side to side,

Denote an empire's giant stride.

Then from the yacht, discourse to sue,

Gay streamers as a signal flew;

And sail made short and helm aport,

Straight the American hove-to.

No need repeat the well-known tale,

How in that ship the exiles sail,

Consigned, by Ferdinand's command,

From Spain to far Columbia's land,

Where they, indeed, in freedom's name,

Blithe welcome from her sons might claim;

But, once the tyrant's leash they slip,

With one accord they seize the ship,

And shape her course—due west before—

For England's nearer northern shore.

Now on the deck were ranged the crew,

For ready service all at hand,

Where'er the captain gave command,

And round, in groups, the exiles drew,

A haggard and a woe-worn band,

Whose faces still displayed the hue

The terrors of the dungeon threw,

And stamped as with a searing brand—

Sad, solemn, mystically grand,

And looking like the soul's adieu

To every hope and every aim

Its mortal sympathies might claim.

One of the number sat apart—

A man advancing into years;

And there was mirrored in the tears,

That ever to his eyes would start,

The image of a broken heart:

A lonely man, wrapped in his sorrows,

And kindred fellowship of horrors—

Like some old house that, by report,

Become a restless ghost's resort—

Or true or false the legend vaunted—

Its ruined look declares it haunted.

He heeded not what passed around,

For still a captive in his mind,

All his perception was confined,

As by a wall's encircling bound,

To what was in those limits found;

And though the day was beaming bright,

He saw nothing round but night;

The fresh and bracing air to him

No freedom brought in breath or limb,

And oft he raised his arm with pain,

As if to ease a cumbering chain.

A throng had to the gangway pressed,

And o'er the side a rope was thrown,

But not a sound his ear addressed;

The shouts, the stir, to him unknown—

Amidst it all, he sat alone.

Nor gives he, from his dungeon breast,

A single glance of interest,

When in two files the crowd divide,

Like a partition of the tide,

And 'twixt the twain appears a maid,

Whom every eye intent surveyed,

And who, with one expansive look,

The round of all the concourse took.

From Lilla broke a poignant cry,

That pain or pleasure might imply,

Or both might haply blended float

In that distracted piercing note—

For when the heart is deeply wrung,

'Tis like an instrument unstrung,

And who from such marred strain can guess

What the emotions 'twould express?

Regardless of inquiries loud,

The maiden darted through the crowd,

And threw herself, with sobs and tears,

   Down at the old man's feet;

At last, he wakes, he sees, he hears—

   The child and father meet,

And with a rapt embrace control

That joyous tumult of the soul.

But Lilla quickly raised her head—

She heard a well-remembered tread;

That step so firm, 'twas Mowbray's own,

Among a hundred 'twould be known:

By her, at least, whose heart elate

Would its approach reverberate.

She took his hand, that hand so kind,

That now her own first thus entwined,

And though those taper fingers pressed

Light as the down on swan's white breast,

They knit above as round a rock

The lichens with their tendrils lock.

Yet in her face there was no trace

Of passion's radiating grace,

Only deep trust and gratitude

With resignation's light subdued,

Save that a shadow, o'er it darting,

Foreshowed the coming pang of parting.

What perils she had undergone

'Twas not a time to dwell upon;

For with the gale the ship must sail,

And, reined in like a restive steed,

The yacht would still not check her speed.

Her thrilling story, in a word,

Her father and the captain heard,

And, while she to her father clave,

The captain hearty welcome gave.

To thank, to bless, the old man tried,

As Mowbray lingered at their side,

But died the accents as they fell,

And hastily they bade farewell.

And he was gone! O! could it be

That face, that form, no more she'd see?

Not till this moment did she know

The lowest tide and depth of woe,

Wherein, as by a flood borne down,

She seem'd to gasp, to sink, to drown.

How could a life so fragile bear

Such an effusion of despair—

The sense of agonizing pain,

The reeling lightness in her brain,

The stifling pressure on her breath,

Upon her heart the chill of death!

But through her soul, and through her frame,

Like lightning flashed a burning flame—

The fervour of her southern clime,

In a volcanic burst sublime.

Forgot, in that gush vehement,

The hundred eyes upon her bent—

Forgot, as though they ne'er had been,

Her father—all the recent scene;

And, rushing to the vessel's side,

Her eye once more the yacht descried,

And Mowbray, too, who waved adieu,

Nor thought, whilst she herself must stay,

He bore her love, her heart, away!

'Tis over now, like the typhoon,

So furious, exhausted soon,

And as she sits beside her sire,

No trace of her bereavement dire,

But in her face a look serene,

Like a religious vow, is seen.

Her father shall be all her care,

His trials and his life she'll share;

Nor shall he know, by outward sign,

What griefs around her heart entwine,

Nor dream a depth of passion flows

Beneath her bosom's calm repose;

But it shall be a hidden thought,

As 'twere a well in holy grot—

A lonely consecrated spot,

By the despairing spirit sought,

When all its powers are overwrought.

And straight she told him of the plan

That through her mind that moment ran:

How she would teach and paint and sing,

And all the little aids she'd bring,

By thrift and industry and gain,

Their future household to maintain.

And he nor care nor toil should know—

Nay, that must be—she'd have it so!

And then she gave so sweet a smile,

As from the world might well beguile

A pilgrim, led by such a hand,

Into the realm of fairy land.

But not their fate, on England's soil,

To earn the exile's bread by toil,

For great events sweep on before

To meet them on the friendly shore,

And as the welcome news they learn,

Italia's voice bids all return.

THE PERILS OF WAR.

On Lombardy's stream-threaded plain,

Become a swamp by endless rain,

A hovel all sequestered stood,

A bank, a landmark, 'mid the flood;

And night, with rolling darkness hung,

Around its deepest shadows flung,

While still the rain came pouring down,

As 'twould the peering gable drown.

Yet not because the night was drear

The housewife moved about with fear;

Nor yet from any idle dread

The solitude and hour might shed:

'Tis rather that vague rumours fly

Of Austrian columns sweeping nigh,

And, where they pass, they leave the mark

Of licence fierce, and vengeance dark.

Nor for herself alone her brow

Is crossed by a deep furrow now:

Her husband to the king has gone,

With Garabaldi is her son;

And oft a thought unbid will rise,

As 'twere a phantom, to her eyes,

And call her to the battle plain,

If e'er she'd either see again.

A step—a knock—a voice subdued

Admission and asylum sued;

And gladly, in this hour of care,

She listened to the touching prayer,

A maid—'twas Lilla—from the storm

Bore in her father's drooping form,

And placed him sinking in a seat

Before she turned the dame to greet.

The matron, who discerned his need,

Some good Montferrat brought with speed,

And noting in the maiden's look

A languor could not be mistook,

The homely table quickly spread

With maccaroni, rice, and bread,

Inviting them with warmth to share

Her simple unpretending fare.

But Lilla in her father's face

More than exhaustion's hue could trace,

And saw the terror left behind

Still present to his harassed mind—

"O! 'twas not he—my father, no!"

In soothing tones she whispered low.

"Because you know he has been sent

From Naples into banishment

For plotting, in the king's last hour,

To raise the Austrian Queen to power,

You think we are no longer free—

In every shadow Branti see!

More likely that, to Austria sold,

He is in strong Verona's hold;

But e'en if here, why such alarm,

When here he's powerless to harm?"

Thus she essayed to calm and cheer

When clattering hoofs broke on the ear,

And clink of spurs and sabres' clang

Before the echoing hovel rang.

" The Austrians !" the housewife said,

With trembling voice and look of dread—

Then as her eye on Lilla fell,

There rose a fear she dared not tell :

" My child, for you I tremble most,

If here they enter, you are lost:

And, hark! they now draw up apace—

Haste! you must seek a hiding-place !"

And Lilla, in her wild alarm,

Clung to the kindly matron's arm,

But, as she met her father's glance,

Still hesitated to advance,

Held back by that sad look of pain

As fixedly as by a chain,

Till her conflicting doubts repressed

She threw herself upon his breast.

"No! no! from you I will not part,

My refuge be your throbbing heart;

And if I find not safety there,

What sanctuary would they spare!"

To fly, indeed, 'twere now too late:

They must together meet their fate,

For with a sudden crash the door

Was hurled in fragments on the floor:

And in the savage troopers burst,

As leaps a torrent—madly first,

And then in an unbroken rush,

That wider spreads with every gush,

Till, surging to and fro like foam,

Their flashing helmets flood the room.

Yet 'midst them all, as in a storm

One cloud is darkest, looms one form;

And Lilla and her father know,

They stand before their deadly foe.

"Aha! we've tracked you—traitor, spy!

Now by the laws of war, you die!

Sir Captain, this, at last, the slave

Who would betray our column brave,

And who from Piedmont's upstart came

To kindle round us treason's flame:

Now here at once—and on this spot—

I claim that he be tried and shot:

The girl, his daughter, may away—

'Twill but her certain fate delay?"

The soldiers gathered closer round,

Their carbines ringing on the ground—

To Lilla's ear a woful sound;

But as her father stood between,

The wreck of all he once had been,

Her love, as by enchantment, gave

The strength to meet, if not. to save;

And though her bearing still was meek,

Though white her lips, and blanched her cheek—

Before the officer could speak,

She drew a passport from her vest

Their true position to attest,

But this, exclaiming that it lied,

The Captain roughly pushed aside;

She might to General Urban go—

To him this precious passport show,

But were it not before the morrow,

Haply, her sire would come to sorrow.

They dragged the old man out by force,

And bound him on a trooper's horse,

And, as they hurried him along,

Lilla was tangled in the throng,

Who crowded round, with banter rude,

And mockery of womanhood,

While in her ear exulting rang

A hiss, as if a serpent stang.

O! 'twas a moment and a sight

That showed our nature in its night,

And woman's in its pure, sweet light,

That, like a star, still shone out clear

Through all the rampant darkness near,

And kept those men of blood at bay

Until the trumpet called away.

With bursting heart and piercing cry,

In an hysteric agony,

The young girl hid her burning face

In the kind housewife's close embrace.

"Alas, sweet child! you must be gone,

These ruffians will return anon;

For, as I stood unnoted by,

Thus your accuser whispered one:

Then, ere too late, dear lady, fly,

And put your trust in Christ on high,

Nor e'en of human aid despair

While time remains to act and dare:

Five miles from hence, 'mid Como's heights,

My son with Garibaldi fights—

Ah! could you reach the general's ear,

He might with aid or counsel cheer;

And, spite this Austrian's cruel threat,

Achieve your father's rescue yet.

The hope her words, though faltering, brought

By Lilla eagerly was caught,

And, like a flash from Heaven sent,

A light to her distraction lent:

Though her emotion to restrain

Only intensified its pain—

Like fire by furnace walls compressed,

It raged more fiercely in her breast.

Yet soothed and calm to outward view,

With thanks and tears she bade adieu,

And from the fated hut withdrew,

Once more in sorrow and in flight,
To brave the terrors of the night.

Nor forth too soon; for, on the wind,
There came the splash of hoofs behind;
And, as the spur pricks on the steed
It gave an impulse to her speed,
But, where might lithest sinews fail,
How woman's feeble strength avail
For long to pass, with step so fleet,
Through the morass that clogged her feet,
Through the darkness and the rain,
That blended with the flooded plain,
And with the raging hurricane—
Confounding in one strife immense
Earth and the warring elements!

And now, exhausted, she must rest:

She casts a wistful look behind,

For thence her father's danger pressed

A magnet's power on her mind:

And nowhere broke the faintest gleam

Whence faith might spring or hope might beam,

Or show that, while it walled her round,

The dark inclosure had a bound.

No speck of light, no beacon, there—

Whence springs, and how, yon sudden glare?

Those fitful gusts of languid flame

That less illuminate than scare,

Like blushes on the cheek of shame,

Rising to show the inward night,

And sinking as they meet the sight!

That hovel was a lowly roof

Thus to be crushed 'neath War's curst hoof.

O! could not kings and armies spare

Such a poor spoil, to woman's prayer?

Say that proud Francis, on his throne,

Will never hear the deed was done!

Who was it loosed those Croat hordes

To plough Italia's soil with swords?

Who sent them forth, in fierce array,

To burn and ravage, smite and slay,

Knowing the spring-time sown with spears

No harvest yields but blood and tears?

He may not hear—he *will* not—no!

A Hapsburg hears not from below;

And who would sway his mind the least,

Must speak as conqueror or priest.

No shade could this poor ruin fling

Upon the Apostolic King;

But, O! the dame who saw it blaze

Might well a cry to heaven raise.

For here she'd come a joyful bride,

Here first had felt a mother's pride,

Here, loved as mother and as wife,

Had passed a tranquil, happy life;

And never had that humble door

Been closed against the honest poor,

But hospitably ope'd and gave

To all who might asylum crave.

And now, I say, her cry had reached,

Where even kings may be impeached,

And would again in time come down,

A thorn in the imperial crown.

Though Lilla knew not of the blow,

That laid the peasant's homestead low,

Confounded by the burst of light,

She hastily renewed her flight,

And with a prayer, and with a vow,

Waded onward through the slough.

So delicate, so young, so fair,

'Twas strange to see what she could bear,

But from her soul—and not its frame,

That wonderful endurance came;

A strength beyond what Nature gave,

A courage that might shame the brave,

Bearing her up by innate power

Through the distraction of this hour.

Ere long a heavy, tramping sound,

Was heard above the wind and rain;

It seemed to shake the sodden ground,

And in a circle break around,

Making a vortex of the plain:

But Lilla, with perception clear,

Its character learnt by her ear,

And knew 'twas coming in her way,

A mighty force, in close array,

With guard in front, and, at each side,

A flanking corps, led by a guide,

That burst in strength o'er fence and field,

The column's bristling living shield.

In haste, she leaped the current strong,

That ran on either side along,

As here, in the wide plain, by chance

She might escape each scout's quick glance,

And, though 'twas a retreat forlorn,

She crouched amid the beaten corn,

And waited, almost in its path,

The coming avalanche of wrath.

For this, as she divined, the force

That never halted on its course,

But through the province madly tore,

From town to town, and door to door;

If here at rest, in motion there,

To overawe, repress, and scare,

And far and wide a panic spread

Where Urban's flying column sped.

Nearer and closer came the tread,

Vibrating o'er the quivering ground,

And on each side and overhead,

For the fierce wind threw back the sound:

And like the waters round a shoal,

In rapid whirl and breakers fleet,

As the successive billows roll,

Round Lilla swept the tide of feet.

Anon a step—a straggling one—

That dragged behind, came on alone,

Drew close, with long and rapid stride,

And, ere she thought, was at her side:

It paused a moment—'twas a year

In the endurance of her fear—

In that suppression of her breath

Suspending her 'twixt life and death,

A moment such as drowning men

Know once—but never know again.

The step passed on, and all had gone,

And with recovered breath and sense,

To Lilla came back confidence,

And she arose, and looked around—

For drooping clouds no longer frowned;

And now her glance could sweep amain

Far over the unbounded plain,

While up above peered out the sky,

Like a clear depth—like woman's eye,

And from the starry camp a scout,

One beaming orb, shone brightly out,

As if to see the plain were clear,

Ere should the heavenly host appear,

And flashed its light on Lilla's mind,

An augury serene and kind.

And yet she could but ill forbode

As slowly she regained the road,

And thought how far she might have sped

In the uncounted minutes fled;

But the remembrance of her aim

A holy inspiration came,

Like angel in the wilderness,

To soothe, to succour, and to bless,

And, as she journeyed, broke the gloom

That hung around her father's doom.

To him there also came relief

Through his accumulated grief,

That, acting with galvanic strain,

Raised up his soul erect again;

And all his dignity of old,

His steadfast look and bearing bold,

K

So long by sorrow overlaid—

Now burst through sorrow's deepest shade,

And made that wreck—that shattered form—

A raft to battle with the storm.

Fettered and bound, in guard-room thrust,

With courage he could now await

The sentence, cruel and unjust,

That soon would lay him in the dust,

Yet thinks of Lilla desolate,

Exposed alone to Branti's hate,

And to avert a doom so dread,

He could almost have wished her dead.

For her—so loved—he still could live,

Though nothing else the world might give;

And Heaven, with its boundless store,

To him, he felt, could give no more,

For God, through Jesu, reconciled,

His world, his Heaven, was his child.

Yet once his country claimed a sigh.

His native isle, so loved, so dear,

Whose valleys soft, whose mountains high,

Gleamed through the vista of a tear:

And as he thought upon her sorrows

One moment he forgot his own,

So vividly arose the horrors

Her prisons masked with walls of stone,

And vainly were his eyes shut fast

As if he would obscure that past,

For only the deep night of age

Can curtain Memory's glaring stage.

And could it be that hosts, at last,

From other realms had come to save,

And met, in battle shock, the blast

That through the land, a whirlwind, drave,

And the embattled might of France,

With Piedmont's arms, would still advance,

And sweep, a flood, from sea to sea,

Till they reclaimed Italia free!

But ne'er for him to dawn the day

That would inaugurate this sway,

When Italy, no more accurst,

Would into new existence burst:

Nor once again to his racked breast

Would his devoted child be pressed,

Until they also from their yoke

In a new life, new world, awoke.

He knew, from what he overheard,

An orderly in haste had spurred

From Branti, with a message brief,

To the brigade's relentless chief,

And that, if deemed by him a spy,

Upon the morrow he would die.

And faster than the flying steed

Impelled to its extremest speed,

With silent, unsuspected tread,

The hours, life's restless coursers, fled.

He had not slept; for through his frame

Consuming fever spread in flame,

And gave a temper to the league

Of raging weakness and fatigue:

And on each agonizing thought

A terror or a pang was brought,

That, by calamities unknown,

Through Lilla's bosom pierced his own.

The morning came—for him the last—

A fairer morning eye ne'er saw:

No scowling cloud, no thunder blast,

Rebuked the devilries of war:

And nature could appear thus bright

When murder stalked in open light!

For now he heard a general stir,

A hasty foot, a clinking spur,

And needed not by words to learn

They marked the orderly's return.

In manacles they lock his hands,

With ruffian haste draw tight his bands,

For orders, from the general brought,

Have, by their tone, a panic wrought,

And they but wait their prisoner slain,

To quit the post and fly the plain.

With manly step, and courage high,

Close guarded, he walked out to die,

And Branti met him at the door

With look malignant as of yore,

And on his lip a lurking smile,

The trophy of a compassed wile,

That when, before God's judgment-seat,

They face to face again shall meet,

Will rise, a witness, to impeach

More sternly—fatally than speech.

Once more he gazed upon the sun,

Whose daily race had scarce begun;

One look threw at the blue expanse,

That like an ocean met his glance,

A sea without a rock or wave—

So to the weary seems the grave,

Where they may lay their throbbing head,

Eternity their downy bed :

And though they bandage o'er his eyes,

In blindness still he sees the skies.

The soldiers are drawn up in line,

And Branti is to give the sign,

As by the officer he stands,

The fatal kerchief in his hands;

But while he draws the moments out

There suddenly is heard a shout,

That seems in every heart to ring—

" For Italy and our brave king!"

And swiftly came 'mid smoke and flame,

With rifle's sure unerring aim,

A bullet to the mark addressed,

It entered Branti's fated breast.

And there his destined victim stood,

His hands clasped on the holy rood,

Not knowing what this din might mean,

That came the grave and him between,

Till, all at once, around him group

A joyous and exulting troop,

Who, 'mid their greetings loud and kind,

His knees, his wrists, his eyes unbind,

And to dispel his last alarms,

Lilla—his child—is in his arms!

THE GENERAL, THE KING, AND THE EMPEROR.

THE corse of Branti was turned o'er,

And from the wound oozed forth the gore

 In gurgles fresh and glowing;

Through the round vent the bullet tore,

 From life's deep conduit flowing;

And on the ground poured out the tide,

With many a cruel murder dyed,

Which, though unheard, with voice suppressed,

Had each its cry to Heaven addressed,

And now, at last, the sentence came

Swift and consuming as a flame:

Ere said a word, ere drawn a breath,

It dealt the bolt, the stroke of death.

Looked on the captain of the band,

His eye denotive of command

For all it beamed with kindly light,

That, like a beacon on a height,

Would animate in need extreme,

By its directing, cheering gleam:

And 'twas a sight to see how all,

Highest to least, and old and young,

The haughty noble and the thrall,

Upon his look, his glances, hung,

So that no trumpet need to call

·When he would on the foeman fall,

For better than its brazen tongue

His eagle gaze a summons flung,

And whoso felt a patriot's flame

Kindled at Garabaldi's name.

He scanned the corse with look of doubt,

Then, stooping, from the dead man's vest,

He plucked a broad sealed letter out,

As 'twere a secret of the breast,

E'en death would suffer not to rest.

Quick o'er the missive ran his eye—

"A thousand crowns I'd freely pay,

The tidings of this Austrian spy

Could I to Piedmont's king convey,

But well I know, my comrades, this

An enterprise we must dismiss,

For not one here unsearched could hie,

By routes the foeman occupy,

To Milan, where, with trump and drum,

The king to-morrow will have come.

Then silent and depressed the band

Draw closer round and doubtful stand,

As though each still would volunteer

Whate'er the risk to meet or fear,

But that the general's words confess

A greater barrier to success,

For at each Austrian post and guard

The way too surely would be barred,

And, stopped and searched, the letter ta'en

The risk they'd brave, and die in vain.

But what their troubled looks expressed

Sprung a resolve in Lilla's breast,

And now her voice the silence broke

As to the general thus she spoke:

"My father's life I'd buy with mine,

This thou hast saved, the other's thine;

And what thou wouldst not think to take

Accept for our dear country's sake,

And by my hand, God's care shall bring

This letter to the gallant king."

Then, rang out clear that praise sincere,

Enthusiasm's unprompted cheer;

But Garabaldi, who could feel.

The claims of nature 'mid his zeal,

And all their harmonies had learned,

From Lilla to her father turned,

And dyed his cheek a crimson glow,

When, mirrored on that face of woe,

He saw, as in a heart unstrung,

What wrongs, what bitter anguish, wrung

For a design so bold and wild

A parent's tender of his child.

"'Tis not a time, though loth to use,

Such noble service to refuse;

But your worn look and air attest

'Tis needful you should first have rest:

Meanwhile, we'll think of a disguise,

And how to shape this enterprise,

And, haply, may some toils evade,

When night shall lend its friendly shade."

Thus spoke the chief, in such a tone

As gave him in each breast a throne;

And his administering sway

'Twas felt a pleasure to obey:

The forethought shown—his care to save,

Fresh confidence to Lilla gave;

And now repose brought strength and hope,

And dreams that, like a horoscope,

Presented, in a range sublime,

The presage of a brighter time.

Too soon is the illusion past,

The hour of action 's come, at last;

And habited in the disguise

Selected for the enterprise—

A country damsel's smart array,

To ward suspicion by display,

She meets the general at the door,

Was counselled, cautioned, cheered once more,

And, learning all he had to tell,

Departed with a kind farewell.

Though swift her steed, his fullest speed

Reserving for her pressing need,

Not to attract a gazing throng,

She first rode leisurely along.

But as the night fell deeper round,

And sky and earth in darkness bound,

And lonelier the silent way,

Where every step through danger lay,

And every object, as she passed,

And every rustle of the blast,

To eye alert and quickened ear,

Might raise a thought of peril near—

Then, giving freedom to the rein,

She bounded o'er the road amain.

And yet, withal, her courage strong

Expanded at the thought of wrong,

That raised, in terrible array,

All the ills of Austrian sway,

The murders and nocturnal raids,

The scourge for matrons and for maids,

Conscription, exile, severed ties,

Suborners, Jesuits, and spies,

Making the yoke so heavy lie,

'Twas a relief, a gain, to die.

On, swiftly on, for mile on mile,

O'er plain and height, through dark defile,

Where such the silence, such the gloom,

It seemed a region 'yond the tomb,

Where never human foot had trod,

And she was there alone with GOD.

And as the Prophet hid his face,

When standing in the holy place,

So, as her mind the thought embraced,

She trembling crossed herself in haste.

And at that moment rose the moon,

With a resplendence opportune,

And, as a priest might show his flock,

Disclosed the Cross upon a rock,

And Christ, our Saviour, nailed thereto,

His head cast down, his side pierced through:

Then drawing up her quivering steed,

She 'lighted on her knee with speed,

And gave GOD thanks, and Mary prayed,

And twice a Paternoster said.

Onward again, in dread no more,

Though Mouza's towers rise dim before,

And seem to warn her to beware

An Austrian post will meet her there;

For she has put her trust in Heaven,

As 'twere an inspiration given,

And every energy to fire,

Cites a thousand memories dire,

That trumpet, with their thousand tongues,

Her own and all her country's wrongs.

Now seen the town, and looms the gate—

Why looks the place so desolate?

Why breaks no challenge, loud and clear,

From sentinel, as she draws near?

Is it a snare for stragglers laid,

A Jesuitic ambuscade?

Dismounting, she leads on her steed,

As o'er a mine the stormers speed,

Not daring even to take breath,

When the next step may light on death,

And at the postern now she stands,

And lifts the latch with trembling hands:

There is the open guard-room door,

But still no sentry walks before;

And, dropped amain her bridle rein,

She softly enters to explore.

Quick throbs her heart, and, at each beat,

Seems to spring upward from its seat,

And as a wave still changing glides,

So swells. her bosom and subsides.

She fears a trap, she knows the cost,

She'll be—she is already lost,

For if the guard be there to meet,

She now has passed beyond retreat,

And, even then, the thought that rose

To whisper of the scourge's blows,

That scandal to the human name,

Spread o'er her cheek a blush of flame.

But moonlight through the window stole,

And in the room showed not a soul,

Though, on the benches, camping ware,

With remnants of the soldiers' fare,

And other relics, might be traced,

Showing the guard had left in haste:

L

It seemed, for aught beside declared,

A chamber in Pompeii bared,

Where vital footprints are so rife,

One scarce conceives there is no life.

But Lilla the enigma read—

The guard—the Austrians—had fled!

O! what a burden, what a weight,

Her heart then seemed to abdicate,

And tears she had refused to grief

Brought her a transport of relief,

As if a gentle shower stole,

Like Mercy's dew, upon her soul.

By terror now no more oppressed,

She lingered for a moment's rest,

But her o'erwrought and weary eyes

Sleep, ere perceived, took by surprise,

And she was wakened in dismay

By the obtruding gaze of day.

Still, all was quiet, all was calm,

No sound to startle or alarm,

For yet the town had not awoke—

But, oh! how soon its sleep had broke

Had it but heard the faintest word

That 'twas delivered from its yoke:

There now, at last, had dawned a day.

When Austria had ceased to sway:

There now, at last, had come a morn

When Italy stood up new-born,

And, though begun on fields of strife,

This morn's a pledge of future life.

In Milan's streets the jubilee

Attained the height of ecstasy;

For there, through many a long year,

The Austrian had ruled by fear,

And kept the city for his liege,

House by house, in closest siege;

And now this leaguer of each hearth

Had broken like the slimmest lath,

Had like a vapour passed away,

Like a shadow, like a spray;

And men who'd gone to rest as slaves

Now rose up free, as from their graves,

Yet hardly dared to realize

What reached their ears and met their e

And from the housetops was proclaimed,

And from the roaring cannon flamed,

By every voice repeated loud

Through the enthusiastic crowd,

That, like a tide, swept down each street

At every turn fresh streams to meet,

But never varying the look

It first on its assembling took,

As joyous as a summer brook,

And freedom's sunshine one might trace

Reflected in each beaming face.

With trumpet blast and beaten drum

The Emperor and King had come;

The Guard and the Zouaves were there

The triumph to adorn and share,

While Piedmont's legions sent their best

To add their lustre to the rest.

And, oh! those cheers, that rose up round,

Might make e'en heroes' hearts rebound,

But nobler sanction of their cause

That Beauty's glances beamed applause,

And flowers were thrown and kerchiefs waved

To those who had such perils braved,

And, on the field, such service done,

When freedom—that great spoil—was won.

The pageant o'er, the city yet

In crowd on crowd exulting met,

And fraternized, the high and low,

In feeling's gushing overflow;

And noble ladies in the street

Embrace the soldiers as they meet:

A worthy meed for gallant deed,

No kingly guerdon half so sweet!

How welcome had the peril seemed,

Could one of such reward have dreamed!

And such a memory to cheer,

How brilliant future fields appear!

Unheeded through the busy throng

Lilla moved wearily along,

And reached, at length, the stately square

Where rises the cathedral fair.

The pile a moment claimed her gaze,

Bursting upon her like a blaze,

Ethereal in every part,

A very cynosure of art.

Its pinnacles and minarets

Throw up a hundred flashing jets,

That, light and soaring, spring amain,

Like a radiance, from the fane.

Below, the windows, tall and lanced,

'Twixt piers abutting, clearly glanced,

Responding to the sun's bright beams

With glimpses of prismatic gleams,

While all around in niches stood

The saints, a holy brotherhood,

Each in his life a shining light

To guide the pilgrim's steps aright,

Though, in the shape the fabric took,

A truer beacon met the look,

The holy cross, in outline pure,

That spiritual cynosure.

The ducal palace—now a king's—

Close to the sacred temple clings,

Like something that had refuge sought

Within the compass of its wings,

Not by its ministry been taught

To rest upon the strong support

A conscience, clear and holy, brings.

Soon Lilla the piazza crossed,

And now the sentinels accost,

And to their challenge she replies

With a report that satisfies.

A watchful aide-de-camp appears,

And more at large her story hears,

Then, bids her follow, and leads on

Through rooms that with resplendence shone,

The camp's and court's caparison;

For marshals and high men of state

Here on the royal captains wait,

In all the pomp and rich parade

That mark their merit and their grade,

But Lilla, wrapt in thought, scarce gave

A glance at this assemblage brave,

Remembering she soon would be

Where must its chiefest bend the knee,

And stars lose all their feeble light

Before the sun absorbs the sight.

She's bid to wait, and 'twas relief,

Unwatched—untended—to remain,

And for a space, though e'er so brief,

Be left to call her thoughts again,

But comes the aide-de-camp amain,

And now the door is open thrown,

He tells her to advance alone,

And, ere her tremor has subsided,

Into the chamber she has glided.

A blindness seemed to strike her eyes,

'Twas but the dazzle of surprise—

A vivid flash, a sudden glare,

For both the royalties were there,

And all her diffidence took wing

Before the Emperor and King.

She held the letter in her hand,

And on the King had fixed her eye,

When he, with an expression bland,

Referred her to his great ally,

And then she met that potent glance,

The guardian, the guard of France,

And scanned that face of mystery,

Whose thoughtful lines are history,

As yet unwritten and unknown,

And there, like signs prophetic, sown,

Portending less the soul's intents
Than a procession of events.

But from this impress to beguile
His face unbent in a faint smile,
Meant to commend and reassure,
And lightening the portraiture.
He read the letter—slowly read,
As one who would not be misled—
"'Tis true," he murmured, "they have fled.
You met no Austrians on your way
As you rode hitherward to-day?"

Her answer was precise and brief,
It satisfied and pleased the chief,
And King Emmanuel praised her zeal
And ardour for the commonweal,

A guerdon—those few words—to her

No royal treasury could confer,

And both the monarchs gave command

That she should still remain at hand,

Until their pleasure should be known,

And by some mark of favour shown.

Again she passed down the saloon,

The object now of every eye,

For through the crowd vague rumours soon

Her deed and daring magnify:

And blushing deep—no blush to stain,

Yet one that tinged her joy with pain,

A beautiful carnation hue,

Yet feverish and shrinking too,

From the gay court with all its glare,

She turned to the cathedral square.

She heard a voice pronounce her name,

And in her heart an echo came

That promptly and at once replied—

Its cadence, soft but deep, the same,

And, ere the sound familiar died,

An officer was at her side;

And Mowbray—for 'twas he—her glance

Seemed for an instant to entrance.

Then both, as chords together swept

By the light touch of an adept,

When a sweet concert is awoke,

In one blithe exclamation broke:

And soon the thrilling tale was told

Each pressed the other to unfold,

With questionings, that still would hear

Whate'er might come from lips so dear,

Though in the mind fresh thoughts arose

Swifter than language could disclose,

And, thus unspoken, seemed to fade,

Like leaves within a forest glade,

That, ere they force their way to light,

The boughs above o'erlapping smite,

For how in such brief space impart

All the exuberance of the heart!

For but a moment, as it seemed,

This burst, this overflow, of gladness,

Through all their words, their gestures, streamed,

For Mowbray's face grew tinged with sadness!

And though he strove in Lilla's sight

To tint this cloud with borrowed light,

And, like a glass, give back to view

The radiance her glances threw, .

Vain were his efforts to conceal,

For all he felt she too must feel,

Instinctively, and like the thrill

Of one ungovernable will.

And thus did silence 'twixt them glide,

Like a chasm, to divide:

Narrow but deep, they could not spread

Above that depth the word unsaid,

And so on either side they stood

An instant's space in that dark mood,

Until a trumpet's blast awoke,

And then the silence Mowbray broke.

"I told you when Italia's right

Was to be won in open fight,

My sword would flash in her array—

That trumpet calls me to the fray:

My troop is marshalled in the square,

My chief, my charger, wait me there,

And I but claimed a brief reprieve

To follow you, and take sad leave—

For something I long thought to say

Upon my heart a burden lay,

And now, as by a coming fate,

'Tis thrown back from my lips elate,

And all they would in haste unfold,

I feel 'twere best remained untold."

A deep unconscious sigh he drew—

" My time's expired—adieu! adieu!"

And here the trumpet's brazen tongue

Far round another summons flung :

He clasped her hand, he dared not raise

His mournful eye to meet her gaze,

The gaze that, bent upon his face,

Seemed all her senses to embrace,

To hear and feel, as well as see,

In its concentred agony.

"Yet stay, O! stay, one moment more—

One fleeting moment, I implore ;

For I would tell you, ere you go—

And yet I cannot—no, no, no!"

And, sobbing, on his breast she sank,

And left those broken words a blank ;

But when his arm around her flew,

With such a swift response, and true,

And clasped her in a fond embrace,

O! then, she raised her burning face,

And yielded to that sweetest bliss,

Love's first intoxicating kiss.

" I've loved you long—yes, from the first,

And, like a blossom early burst,

My passion 'neath a shade have nurst;

For, while you leant upon my care,

I could not urge a lover's prayer,

And now, when we have met again,

There still was something to constrain :

My love I scrupled to confess,

Since at this hour 'twould but distress,

Could I have hoped to win your heart,

To snatch it up, and then depart.

But I have won it—yes, 'tis mine,

I feel it with my own entwine ;

And, oh ! it brings so sweet a joy

Not parting even can alloy :

There, sweet, adieu!—what rapture this!"

Again—again—the fervent kiss;

But the fierce trumpet to obey,

He forced—he tore himself away.

PART THE EIGHTH.

SOLFERINO.

THE battle rages far and wide,

On the broad plain and steep hill side,

On rock and slope and river bank,

On Solferino's jutting flank,

From Peschiera on the right,

To Goito's flat road the fight

A dozen miles breaks on the sight;

And twice two hundred thousand blades,

In flashes, like long trails of light,

Rose through the smoke of cannonades,

Then sank, as in the gulf of night,

Or, gleaming through its depths, became

Reflectors to the forks of flame,

And trump and drum and ringing cheer

Deafen from every side the ear,

With musketry's prolonging roll,

The requiem of many a soul,

Completing, with the cannon's roar,

The awful orchestra of war.

In the centre, from a height,

Napoleon directs the fight

For France and Italy allied,

And battling nobly, side by side,

While Austria's Emperor is found

On Cavriana's towering ground,

The centre, too, of the array

That served his cause this bloody day,

Fighting with all its might and main,

On hill and slope and death-swept plain,

So that the beam, whence triumph hung,

Now up, now down, uncertain swung,

And Piedmont's monarch, on the left,'

From his ally was fiercely cleft,

And though he bravely struggled still

On San Martino's rugged hill,

Now on its crest, now driven back,

And now renewing the attack—

Although the dead and wounded round

Spread like a pavement o'er the ground,

And from the church—perversion dire!—

And from the ridge, poured sheets of fire,

And grape and balls, with fearful crash,

As up the fatal slope they dash,

M

To meet upon its bristling crown

That wave of steel that hurls them down:

And Mollard's corps, brought up in haste,

Is in the front of conflict placed,

And twice breaks through that barrier dense,

And caps the frowning eminence,

And twice is driven back again,

And thrown in fragments on the plain.

Then Cucchiari's column sweeps,

Like a tornado, up the steeps,

And, through the smoke and through the fire,

Bursts on the Austrians entire,

And seems, with its resistless rush,

Their broken ranks at last to crush,

Propelling them right down the hill

In wild disorder, fighting still.

But suddenly, with loud huzza,

They form once more a living bar,

The bayonets, the sabres flash,

And foe meets foe in awful crash,

And men fall down like trodden reeds

Beneath the hoofs of rushing steeds,

Which here, without a rider, fly,

Here masterless dash madly by,

And here, like heroes, stand and die.

Thus, hour by hour, through all the day,

The Austrian legions stood at bay,

And, though unable to defeat,

Forced the Sardinians to retreat.

'Twas but a moment—but a pause,

The lull that more than tempest awes

By the uncertainty intense

That keeps the spirit in suspense,

For Fanti's column now is sent

To win that mountain battlement.

.

But on the right the deadly fight

   More fiercely still is waged,

For there the bulk of Austria's might

   With France herself's engaged;

And there—erect, detached, alone—

High Solferino rears its cone

Like fabled Pluto's sulphur throne,

Or rather as itself a god,

The battle hanging on its nod—

For who should last possess its crest,

With him the victory would rest.

Though volleys roar, and cannon's flame,

As swift as lightning, went and came,

Above the smoke, above the fight,

A tower on that lofty height

Looked o'er the country like an eye,

Further than mortal glance could fly,

From where the Alps throw up their chain

Far as the Po, a boundless plain.

That stronghold seemed to stand secure,

Amid the conflict, safe and sure,

A sanctuary and a keep,

Surmounting precipices steep,

That rose all round from plateaux three,

The strong position's core and key,

Alive with strife in every part,

The battle's palpitating heart.

For here, where two great armies meet,

It bounds, it rocks, with every beat,

As could the mass of granite feel

The mighty shock of fire and steel.

Napoleon from a jacent rise [10]

Surveys the fight with piercing eyes,

And as he sees occasion claim,

With Cyclop's force and marksman's aim,

And with traditionary ken,

He launches thunderbolts of men,

And though recoiling shivered back,

They fly again to the attack,

Re-form, unite, and onward bear

Once more to meet the foeman there,

Once more before the raining fire—

Not to retreat, but to retire.

Each feels within his breast the sway

One mind infuses through the fray,

And spreading over all the field,

It seems to each a special shield—

A mighty influence to wield!

For where Napoleon bids advance,

There, through the smoke, the columns glance,

And with a shout for him and France—

O'er mangled heaps of comrades slain

They rush upon the foe again.

But now above the conflict broke

A louder roar than it awoke—

The mighty God of battles spoke!

And from the Heavens came his thunder

As if 'twould rend the hill asunder,

And o'er the dark and frowning sky,

The lightnings, blue and arrowed, fly,

Like trains that, quickened by the gale,

Fire the artillery of hail:

But still, through all the storm, the fight

Continues on that blood-washed height,

And D'Hilliers, Forey, Camou there

The dangers of their soldiers share,

Again and yet again lead on

Against the Church's garrison,

Against the houses, loopholed all,

That round the winding passes crawl—

Against the cemetery wall,

Till, in support, fresh legions come

With ringing cheer and beat of drum,

And through the vineyards on the steep

The Guard with force resistless sweep.

Lebœuf, exposed to their full brunt,

Takes the batteries in the front,

With the artillery of the Guard,

While onward Forey presses hard,

And gallantly the Austrian host

Defended, hand to hand, the post.

But now by a bold charge, and now

Foot by foot, on the hill's brow,

The eagles of the French advance,

The church displays the flag of France;

They win the village, win the height,

The Austrians recede from sight,

But, when the smoke has cleared away,

The French perceive them still at bay,

And, pushing on, each rising mound

Becomes another battle-ground.

And here was Mowbray helpless lying,

Among the wounded and the dying,

No strength to move, no voice to cry

For help, if even help were nigh:

He saw the day was waning fast—

For him—and many more—the last,

For how live through the coming night?

O! better to have died in fight!

This burning thirst, this throbbing pain,

His gory couch of comrades slain,

His charger fallen at his side—

Ah! would he then himself had died!

But, after he had long repined,

A better spirit swept his mind,

And raised a Christian trust and hope ˙

With suffering and pain to cope—

Admonishing by many a groan,

From those so thick around him strown,

No murmurs in his breast should rise

When others shared the sacrifice.

But whence that step, and whose that voice,

That make him, 'mid his pangs, rejoice?

And when he hears that bitter cry,

Why does he feel he must not die?

'Tis Lilla—yes, he knows, 'tis she,

Though her sweet face he cannot see,

And now what evil can betide?

He's saved—he's guarded by his bride!

*　　　*　　　*　　　*

Two months had passed, and Mowbray now,

To health restored, redeemed his vow,

And Lilla, his in death or life,

Became indeed his bride—his wife.

NOTES.

[1] [Murder and theft their station took,
By royal licence free to act,
The town to harass and distract.]

This statement may appear incredible. There is, however, ample testimony to prove that convicted brigands, and other malefactors, were released from prison by the late King of Naples, and let loose on his subjects, with the view of distracting public attention from political affairs by the disorders which these ticket-of-leave ruffians might be expected to create.

[2] [There was the Criminalli door.]

The Criminalli is, as its name imports, the criminal prison, where persons charged with political offences are confined, together with felons, from their first arrest.

[3] [Like figures in old Egypt's caves.]

The allusion is not to the tableaux and bas-reliefs of the Egyptian structures, but to the figures which, in the older rock temples, project from the excavated walls, and seem to sustain the roof.

4 [Or friars niched in standing graves.]

An allusion to a practice very prevalent in Sicily, and, indeed, in other parts of Southern Europe. At Malta I visited a Capuchin monastery, in the village of Florian, where the skeletons of the defunct abbots were all ranged in niches round a vaulted chapel, arrayed in the same woollen gown and cowl they had worn during life.

5 [But only quarried pits were there.]

This cemetery is described from one actually seen by the author, and the description may indeed be applied to too many in the kingdom of the Two Sicilies, and even other countries of Southern Europe.

6 [As warned of yore the sea-cliff bell.]

Before the introduction of lighthouses, a huge bell, suspended from a beam, was erected at dangerous points of the coast, and, swung by the wind, warned the mariner, through the obscurity of night or fog, of the vicinity of the shore.

7 [Not art the granite way had made,]

The roads of Sicily owe little indeed to art. Even the two principal towns, Palermo and Messina, are not connected by a road; and so jealous is the government of any facilities for popular intercourse, that the roads communicating with the interior do not extend beyond thirty miles.

[8] [She first rode leisurely along.]

The adventure ascribed to Lilla finds a counterpart in the following incident of the war, quoted from the Milan correspondence of the *Times*, December 22, 1859 :—

"The marriage of Garibaldi gains more and more consistency. It is quite a romantic story. When General Urban advanced with overpowering forces, the Cacciatori delle Alpi had to abandon their position on the Lago di Como, and fell back towards Varese. The town of Como and all the neighbourhood were in consternation on the prospect of a visit from the Austrians; the *employés*, and all those who were for one reason or another against the movement which had taken place, were raising their heads; the mass, timid and without organization, was what masses under these circumstances usually are; and yet it was important to inform Garibaldi of the state ¡of things, and to give him likewise details about the position of the Austrians. But there was no one who would expose himself to the risk of undertaking this ticklish embassy. A young lady, not twenty-two, the daughter of a neighbouring proprietor, offered herself, and partly on horseback and partly on foot, succeeded, by circuitous mountain roads, in reaching Garibaldi's camp. The general had gone out with his chief of the staff to the outposts when they met the courageous young lady, who not only delivered her message but took back another equally successfully. This was the beginning of their acquaintance. After his resignation, Garibaldi went to visit the lady's family at their country place, near the Lake of Como; his visit was to have been only short, but by a strange coincidence he had, shortly after his arrival, a fall with his horse, in which he hurt his knee, and which obliged him to remain in the house."

⁹ [And Piedmont's monarch on the left.]

The conflict at San Martino is thus described in the French official account :—

" On its part the Piedmontese army, placed on our extreme left, had also had a rude and splendid day's work. It was advancing in four divisions in the direction of Pescheira from Pozzolengo and Madonna della Scoperta, when, at about 7 in the morning, its advanced guard encountered the enemy's advanced posts between San Martino and Pozzolengo. The combat commenced, but strong Austrian reinforcements hurried up and drove the Piedmontese further back than San Martino, even threatening to cut off their line of retreat. A brigade of Mollard's division then arrived in all haste on the scene of combat, and assaulted the heights on which the enemy had established themselves. Twice it attained the summit, and possessed itself of several pieces of cannon; but twice also it had to yield to numbers, and to abandon its conquest.

"The enemy was gaining ground, in spite of some brilliant charges of the King's cavalry, when Cucchiari's division, debouching in the field of battle by the road of Rivoltella, came to support General Mollard. The Sardinian troops rushed forward a third time with impetuosity under a murderous fire ; the church and all the works raised on the right were carried, and eight pieces of cannon were taken. But the enemy again succeeded in disengaging the cannon and in retaking the positions.

"At this moment the 2nd brigade of General Cucchiari, which had been formed in columns of attack to the left of the Lugano road, marched against the church of St. Martino, regained the lost ground, and carried the heights for the fourth time, without holding them, however; for, overwhelmed by volleys of grape, and facing an enemy who was constantly receiving reinforcements and incessantly returning to the charge, it could not hold out till the arrival of succour from General Mollard's 2nd Brigade, and the Piedmontese, being quite exhausted, retreated in good order along the Rivoltella road.

"It was then the Aosta Brigade of Fanti's division, which had at first gone towards Solferino to form a junction with Marshal Baraguay d'Hilliers, was sent by the King to support Generals Mollard and Cucchiari in the attack on San Martino. That body was checked for a while by the storm ; but about five o'clock in the evening this brigade and the Pignerol one, supported by a numerous artillery, marched on

N

the enemy under a terrible fire and reached the heights.
They took possession of them foot by foot, field by field, and
managed to hold them by very desperate fighting. The
enemy began to give way, and the Piedmontese Artillery,
gaining the ridge, soon crowned it with twenty-four pieces
of cannon, which the Austrians vainly endeavoured to cap-
ture ; two brilliant charges of the King's cavalry dispersed .
them ; volleys of grape threw their ranks into confusion, and
the Sardinian troops finally remained masters of the formid-
able positions which the enemy had defended for a whole day
with such obstinacy."

10 [Napoleon from a jacent rise.]

The following paragraphs from the French official account
describe the attack on the height of Solferino :—

" These measures having been taken, the Emperor repaired
to the heights, in the centre of the line of battle, where Marshal Baraguay d'Hilliers, too distant from the Sardinian
army to be able to act in conjunction with it, had to struggle
in very difficult ground against troops which were incessantly
renewed.

" The Marshal had nevertheless arrived at the foot of the
steep hill on which the village of Solferino is built. That
village was defended by considerable forces, intrenched in an
old château and a large cemetery, both of which were sur-
rounded by thick and crenelated walls. The Marshal had
already lost a great number of men, and had had more than

once to expose himself by leading on the troops of Bazaine's and Ladmirault's divisions. Worn out with fatigue and heat, and exposed to a heavy fire of musketry, these troops gained ground with much difficulty. At this moment the Emperor ordered Forey's division to advance, one brigade on the side of the plain, and the other on the height against the village of Solferino, and caused it to be supported by Camou's division of light infantry of the Guard. He caused to advance with these troops the artillery of the Guard, which, under the command of General de Sevelinges and General Lebœuf, took up an uncovered position of about 300 mètres from the enemy. This manœuvre decided the success in the centre. While Forey's division seized on the cemetery, and General Bazaine dashed his troops forward into the village, the light infantry and riflemen of the Imperial Guard climbed up to the foot of the tower commanding the château and possessed themselves of it. The little hills near Solferino were successively carried, and at half-past three the Austrians evacuated the position, under the fire of our artillery, placed on the crests, and left in our hands 1,500 prisoners, 14 pieces of cannon, and two colours. The share of the Imperial Guard in this glorious trophy was 13 guns and one colour."

THE END.

LONDON :

PRINTED BY W. CLOWES AND SONS, STAMFORD STREET
AND CHARING CROSS.

www.ingramcontent.com/pod-product-compliance
Lightning Source LLC
Chambersburg PA
CBHW030638030726
47497CB00006B/1853